THE LAST TITAN: UNLEASHED

CHRIS SKULL

The Last Titan: Unleashed

By Chris Skull

Content Warning

This novel contains depictions of graphic violence that may be disturbing to some readers. Reader discretion is advised.

Published by Chris Skull and Hephaistos' Workshop

Ermou 71, Thessaloniki 55632, Greece

This is a work of fiction. All characters, organizations, and events portrayed in this novel are either products of the author's imagination or are used fictitiously. Any resemblance to actual persons, living or dead, or actual events is purely coincidental.

First Edition

December 2025

ISBN: 9786180060164

Cover Design by Amanda M

Graphic Design by Apostolos Katsikas

For inquiries regarding bulk purchases, special editions, or other requests, please contact:

Email: info@the-last-titan.com

Website: www.the-last-titan.com

Printed on recycled paper with eco-friendly inks, in support of sustainable publishing practices.

To the love of my life—my muse, my anchor, my spark—whose presence echoes like prophecy in every word I write, and whose love endures storm and flame…

The Last Titan: Unleashed

CONTENTS

CHAPTER ONE
THE LONG WAY BACK

The first light of dawn crept through the tall forest, chasing away the lingering chill as its warmth spread to the outskirts of Dion.

The hamlet, still shrouded in the remnants of night, lay only a short distance away.

Heracles rose and stretched, a low groan escaping him as the stiffness in his muscles protested with every movement.

His eyes landed on the bow and shield he had acquired only recently. The soft glow of morning light played across the intricate details of each piece, revealing the weaponsmith's exceptional craftsmanship. A deep sorrow stirred within him, knotting his stomach and tightening his chest. He examined each item closely, brushing his fingers over the fine engravings and flawless lines, marveling at the artistry. But their beauty only deepened the ache—a cruel reminder of the price paid to obtain them.

That ache lingered as he gathered the gear, his movements slow and measured. He turned his attention to Prometheus, who slept peacefully against the rough bark of a tree. It still felt unreal to him—this man, old and frail, was indeed the great Prometheus. The last of his kind. The Titan who had defied the gods and sacrificed everything for mortals.

Now, he was but a shadow of his former self—weak, aged, and struggling even with the simplest tasks, like lifting an apple to his lips. Yet Heracles saw something indescribable. Something ancient. A glimmer of raw, unmeasured power buried beneath the weight of his suffering. It was a power only a Titan could possess: the primordial grace of divinity—vast and untamed—lingering even in the twilight of his existence.

"Prometheus, it's time," he said, reaching out to shake him gently by the shoulder. But before his hand could make contact, a sharp whistling sound tore through the air. An arrow whizzed past him and slammed into the tree bark, mere inches from Prometheus' face. The violent thud of its impact jolted the old Titan awake. He opened his eyes—almost devoid of color, though a faint shade of blue had begun to emerge—and stared at the arrow, still quivering from the force of the strike.

Heracles spun, his keen vision scanning the trees. A second arrow hurtled toward them, but this time he was ready. With a swift, fluid motion, he unsheathed his sword and deflected the arrow, sending it spinning harmlessly away from their position.

"Show yourself!" Heracles shouted, his voice steady. "You had your chance, and you missed. Face me."

Between the tall trees, a figure emerged, moving slowly, fading in and out of sight as it passed behind the trunks.

"What makes you think I missed?" came the whisper—soft, but sharp. "This was just a warning, after all."

"Who are you?" he asked, his voice calm as he patiently waited for the figure to draw closer. His sword was in hand, ready for whatever might come, though he could already feel her presence—her essence, her divinity.

"I am the mistress of these woods, and you have trespassed on sacred ground. You stole what was never yours, struck down my cherished Nereids—the guardians of the Gate—and claimed their weapons as spoils. But most grievously, you freed one who should have remained imprisoned. I knew someone like you was here; I simply could not believe it. Well done avoiding detection."

"I appreciate the compliment. Now, how about you tell me exactly who you are and what you want," he said, tightening his grip on the sword.

The figure stopped a few yards away and locked eyes with him. Her eyes differed only slightly in shade from Heracles' rich, luminous green—but as he had suspected, they were devoid of pupils, an unmistakable mark of her divinity.

"My name is Artemis. Well met, brother," she said, slinging her bow over her shoulder.

Heracles was struck by her wild beauty. Her pale, flawless, almost statue-like skin accentuated her light brown hair, a cascade of rebellious curls framing her small, exquisitely detailed face. The faint scars scattered across her features only heightened her allure, making her beauty dangerously captivating.

"It was you before, right?" Heracles asked, though he already knew the answer.

"It was," Artemis replied, nodding slightly in respect, a hint of admiration in her tone. "Like I said—masterfully done with the apples."

Unlike the Nereids or the guards of Pantheon, Artemis wore no armor. Instead, she was clad in a tunic that seemed woven from moss, its earthy texture and deep green hues blending her seamlessly with the forest—as though nature itself had embraced her divinity. Her presence, like her curls, was untamed yet purposeful: the very embodiment of the huntress she was born to be.

"What do you want, Artemis?" he asked, casting a quick glance at Prometheus, who sat silently, unmoving.

"You know exactly what I want. I can temporarily overlook all your indiscretions—except one," Artemis said, her stare fixed on Prometheus.

"It is done," he replied, his voice carrying a determination as unyielding as the mountains.

"I wish we had met under different circumstances. Truly, I have always wanted to meet you, Heracles," Artemis said, slowly unslinging her bow. "However, it seems your mind is made up—and unfortunately, we all have our duties."

Heracles stepped in front of Prometheus, positioning himself as a shield against the imminent threat, and offered him a reassuring nod. At the same time, Artemis slowly nocked an arrow and took a measured step back. Several long heartbeats passed in silence, broken only by the wind whistling through the green canopy above.

"Let us see if the rumors are true, then," Artemis said. In a flash, she drew the string and released the arrow at Heracles. Though he was ready to fight, her speed was so extraordinary—and the distance between them so short—that even he could not react in time. The arrow struck his upper leg, piercing straight through. The bloodied tip jutted from the back of his thigh, glinting faintly in the dappled forest light.

Heracles glanced down at his leg, noting how the arrow's tip had come to rest only a short distance from Prometheus. For a brief moment, he wondered whether the shot had been meant for the Titan or for himself—but Artemis gave him no time to dwell on it. She had already nocked another arrow.

Heracles hurled his sword with precision, the blade spinning toward Artemis as he charged forward. But before he could reach her—or the sword could find its mark—she spun gracefully, evading both. A second arrow flashed from her bow and struck him in the shoulder, but he did not stop. With a thunderous impact, he barreled into her, sending Artemis tumbling onto the soft forest floor.

"I am still not convinced," Artemis said, lifting her head slowly while gripping her bow.

"We don't have to do this," Heracles responded, unfazed by the two arrows embedded in his body.

"You are right, we do not—yet we will," she countered, then dashed behind a tree.

As Artemis disappeared from sight, he quickly returned to Prometheus, picked up the shield, and placed it in his hands.

"Hold this. Protect yourself. And don't worry—I've got this," he said, offering Prometheus a reassuring smile.

Heracles grabbed the bow and quiver, then sprinted off to face Artemis, scooping up his sword from the ground as he went. Taking cover behind a tall tree, he pulled the arrows from his flesh, relieved they had missed anything vital. He leaned out from the trunk, eyes scanning the foliage.

An arrow struck the tree mere inches from his face, scattering a burst of bark and dust into his eyes, momentarily blurring his vision. It took a few heartbeats for his sight to clear—just in time to glimpse Artemis darting through the forest before vanishing behind another tree.

The realization dawned on him—he was trapped, hunted by none other than the Goddess of the Hunt. This was her territory, her domain, and he was at a disadvantage he had not anticipated. Even so, there was no other option. She had given him no choice. It had to be done. He had to close the distance.

Without a second thought, he leapt from cover and sprinted forward. The next arrow barely missed him. He slammed into another tree trunk, shaking pinecones loose from its branches. As he attempted to repeat the maneuver, an arrow struck one of the falling pinecones, splitting it mid-air. Redirected, the arrow grazed Heracles before embedding itself in the ground.

With the Nereid's bow—polished silver and sturdy oak—in hand, he knelt by the tree, leaning against its trunk, and closed his eyes. He held his breath and focused, shutting out every other sound. Moving was no longer an option; he could not win this fight by playing her game. Yet he heard nothing. Her movements were silent, stealthy—utterly devoid of even a whisper. She was, after all, the perfect huntress.

Yet he could feel her presence—she was close. He opened his eyes and instinctively fired an arrow, catching her by surprise as she crept through the forest. The arrow sliced past her as she dove behind a tree for cover.

He nocked another arrow and drew the cord to its limit, the bow creaking under the immense pressure, as if on the verge of breaking. He let it fly. The arrow tore through the air with such speed that the sound seemed unable to catch up. It struck the tree with a loud thump and punched clean through. A faint cry came from behind the trunk, spurring Heracles to rush toward it.

Certain yet cautious, he approached Artemis' cover, only to find her immobilized, her back resting against a younger, slender tree. It was a cruel twist of fate: caught off guard by his first shot, she had taken refuge behind a trunk too narrow to shield her. Her bow lay discarded on the ground, and her shooting hand hung limp. Though there was no visible wound, her expression said it all—her fight was over.

"You are a worthy opponent. I am impressed—it seems, for once, the rumors were true," Artemis said, spitting blood onto the pine needle-covered ground.

Heracles slung the bow over his shoulder and placed a hand on the sword's hilt. He met her gaze, the weight of his decision already forming in his mind.

"Pass my regards to Prometheus. It seems he now has a protector worthy of a Titan—or at least of a once-Titan," she said, smiling as blood began to drip from her mouth. "There is no need to drag this out. Finish it."

Heracles slowly drew his sword, his focus never leaving Artemis, and stepped to her side. Gripping the blade with both hands, he raised it high as she closed her eyes, bracing for the blow. With unwavering precision, he brought the sword down—the blade grinding against the bark until it severed the arrow that held her fast to the tree.

Freed from the tree's grasp, Artemis crumpled to her knees, her defiance draining away as blood seeped from her wound, leaving a dark stain on the bark.

"That is all I can offer. The rest is yours to manage," Heracles said as he sheathed his sword.

Artemis raised her head and met his gaze. He stood before her—a demigod—his expression sincere, his strength tempered by compassion. She was truly impressed. This was not the kind of strength she had expected from someone like him—especially not mercy. Hatred, perhaps. Vengeance. But not this.

"Yet again, masterfully done, brother," she murmured, her voice faltering as unconsciousness claimed her. "Until our next meeting."

CHAPTER TWO
TRUST UNSPOKEN

They reached the central square of Dion, greeted by the bustling sounds of the hamlet stirring to life. Heracles, with Prometheus ever at his side, caught a few skeptical glances from the nearby residents. Yet he paid them no mind, striding toward the local tavern with purposeful steps. Hunger gnawed at him, and the thought of a proper breakfast quickened his pace. Though it was early, and he feared the meal might be delayed, fortune smiled upon him—the tavern door was already ajar.

He set down his equipment and guided Prometheus to a seat at the same outdoor table where he had once enjoyed a satisfying meal. Though it had been only recently, the memory felt distant—like something from a life no longer his.

"They will never stop," Prometheus whispered.

"What?" Heracles asked, his brow furrowing.

"They will not stop. Not ever. They will hunt us to the edge of the world," he said, holding Heracles in an unrelenting stare.

"Let them try," he countered as he lowered himself into a seat.

"You are his son, are you not?" Prometheus asked, his expression darkening with a faint flicker of resentment.

"Heracles!" called the young woman as she darted out of the tavern, cutting their conversation short.

"By the grace of Zeus, you're back! It's a pleasure to see you again. And you've brought a friend this time." She smiled warmly, brushing a loose strand from her cheek, then added, "My name is Melite. My apologies for never introducing myself before."

She extended her hand to Prometheus, but he did not seem to notice her, his sight still fixed intently on Heracles.

"Pleased to officially meet you, Melite. You'll have to pardon my companion—he's very tired," Heracles said, returning her smile.

"Think nothing of it; I'm just glad you're well," she replied, her smile gentle yet radiant, carrying a charm that seemed to brighten the moment.

Her hair, soft and faintly scented of lavender, brushed against Heracles' skin as she leaned closer, her whisper punctuated by a light, teasing chuckle: "I've had my share of grumpy elders."

"So, what will it be, dear guests?" Melite asked with a playful wink at Heracles, who, to his surprise, found himself winking back. "You know what? I think I already do. Leave it to me."

He watched her retreat into the tavern, her presence lingering like a warm breeze. Once she disappeared inside, he turned his attention back to Prometheus, who was still staring at him.

"Yes, I am," he stated. Prometheus did not respond; he simply continued to pierce him with his faintly blue eyes.

"Listen," Heracles continued, his voice steady, "I know what you're thinking, and no, it's not that. Maybe part of it is, but you do not know the whole story. Tell you what—when you're ready to talk, I will too. I'll answer anything you want to know. But until then, trust me. We're in this together now. Does that sound fair?"

Prometheus' gaze lingered, unwavering, before he finally turned away. In the soft morning light, his weathered, almost broken face was fully revealed. His silence hinted at wounds too deep to voice. Heracles marveled at the Titan's endurance, recognizing the immense strength it took to survive such agony. Earning his trust would not be easy, but Heracles knew one thing with certainty: Prometheus had no choice but to rely on him.

Colchis lay hundreds of miles away, and even under perfect conditions, the journey back would take at least two months—if not longer. A horse could shorten the journey, but few places along the way offered the chance to acquire one, and the cost would demand sharp bargaining.

The ideal way to travel was by sea, yet few captains dared to brave the Sea of Helle. Treacherous reefs and shifting shallows lay in wait beneath the surface, while towering waves battered the unwary. A dense, blinding mist cloaked the waters, veiling every danger in an unrelenting shroud of peril.

This, however, was a problem for another time. The growling of his stomach pulled him back to the present, just as Melite stepped through the tavern door.

"I brought fresh water and some local wine, as I'm sure you're thirsty from your journey. The food will follow shortly—I suspect someone is quite famished," she said, her playful tone accompanied by a lighthearted smile.

"Where did you go? You sounded so dramatic before," she added, setting the amphorae on the table. "Oh, pray forgive me—I did not mean to intrude," she murmured, her expression softening into one of shyness.

"It's fine; it was a bit dramatic, you're right. Though, I think it is best not to disclose the specifics. It is safer that way," Heracles said, offering an apologetic smile.

"Don't be silly. I was just curious, and I am sure it was something very important and personal, so I completely understand your reluctance to share," she said, placing two kylixes on the table. "I'll be back shortly with your breakfast."

As Melite disappeared once more into the tavern, he turned his attention to Prometheus, who had unceremoniously fallen asleep at the table. His arms were folded beneath his head, his breathing steady but heavy.

"This will be a long journey," he murmured, his voice low as his gaze drifted toward the distant horizon.

CHAPTER THREE
THE WHISPERED TRUTH

The sun began its languid descent behind the shadowed heights of Mount Olympus, casting the hamlet in a golden glow as preparations for the night unfolded. It was a quiet, somewhat secluded village, perched just far enough from the coastline to offer a sense of serenity, yet elevated enough to command a breathtaking view of Pieria's sprawling beauty.

Seated by the small, second-floor window of the tavern, Heracles let the waning light carve sharp shadows across his rugged features. He lit his pipe, its fragrant smoke curling lazily upward, blending with the cool evening breeze.

Initially, he had been reluctant to linger so near Mount Olympus—especially after recent events—but Melite had been persuasive. Her charm, as always, proved irresistible, and he had at last relented. Besides, Prometheus could use a good night's rest in a proper bed.

From his perch, he watched a small procession of villagers lead a modest flock of sheep toward the altar of Zeus. The animals, blissfully unaware of their impending fate, followed docilely, their soft bleats rising into the evening air. Such rituals were a common sight in a village nestled at the foot of the sacred slopes of Mount Olympus.

He drew deeply from his pipe once more, then exhaled slowly, releasing a plume of smoke that twisted and swirled through the fading light. The last rays of sunlight pierced the haze, creating a fleeting, ethereal dance in the air.

He glanced at his wounds, now carefully bandaged after Melite's insistent care—her refusal to take no for an answer was as unwavering as ever. His shoulder felt much improved, though his leg remained stiff. Limping was a luxury he could scarcely afford, especially with the long journey to Colchis still ahead. Even so, he counted himself fortunate: the arrows had inflicted only minor damage.

Although he still harbored doubts about whether returning was the wisest choice, the overwhelming need to reunite with Medea silenced any lingering hesitation. After all, no place lay farther from here—nor could any other offer the aid he so desperately required. And if anyone could remove the curse from Prometheus, it was her. Then there was Podargos—his trusted steed and steadfast companion—awaiting him, along with the weight of a promise he had yet to fulfill to Ladon.

As the hours slipped by and the muted glow of the night sky enveloped the hamlet, Heracles rose from his bed, sleep elusive. Quietly, he checked on Prometheus, who lay deep in slumber, his breathing steady, yet still heavy. Gently, he draped another blanket over him, halting as faint murmurs escaped the Titan's lips. Leaning in closer, he strained to discern the words—their melody celestial and otherworldly—yet they danced just beyond his comprehension. The language was divine, but not one he had mastered. It was not for lack of knowledge or ability; it was a matter of choice.

All his life, he had sought to keep his distance from the divine, resisting the pull of fate that bound him to the gods. He had yearned for a quieter life—one free of glory, riches, or divine entanglement. Yet fate had other plans, and each time he strayed from its course, misfortune followed like a shadow that never loosened its grip. Now, resigned to what must be done, he would see it through. Perhaps, when it was over, rest would come at last—a long-overdue reward, and one he would accept without protest.

He grabbed his cloak and sword before descending the narrow stairs to the tavern's ground floor. The room was cloaked in darkness, the faint, lingering scent of roasted meat the only reminder of the evening's bustle. Stepping outside, he pulled the door shut behind him and quickened his pace toward the northern edge of the village. The streets were steeped in stillness, the empty paths whispering of a world retreating into slumber.

Guided by the moon's pale glow, he reached the village outskirts—near the place where Artemis had shattered their fragile peace. The eerie silence of the forest, coupled with the biting chill of the night, sent a shiver across his skin as he pushed through the dense undergrowth. When he reached the tree, he found nothing but the dark stain of blood marring its trunk—Artemis was gone.

A weight lifted from his chest; she was neither nearby nor dead. This must have been a test—it was no coincidence that her arrows had spared his life. She had simply wanted to gauge his skill. If she had desired, she could have ended him easily, right then and there—but she had not. While this seemed a logical conclusion, he could not fully grasp her reasoning. Yet the truth was becoming clearer: this was not merely about his ability, but about something deeper—perhaps a lesson, or a glimpse into her character. He was beginning to see that not all gods were the same—no more uniform in their nature than mortals.

However, it was time to leave this place behind; it would not take long for news of Prometheus' escape to reach the ears of the gods. As he had warned, their hunters would not relent. They needed to move on—and quickly—putting as much distance between themselves and the village as possible. The sooner, the better.

A faint rustle echoed behind Heracles, snapping him into a defensive stance. His hand moved instinctively to his sword, drawing it slowly as he remained still—alert and ready. Then came a sharp crack of twigs, shifting his attention to a nearby shadow. Sword in hand, he began to move, his steps as silent as possible in the hushed gloom of the night-shrouded forest. The oppressive presence of the trees seemed to press in around him. Another shuffle, closer this time, spurred him into action. He rushed toward it, but before he could reach its source, a figure stepped out from behind a tree.

It was Melite.

“What are you doing here?” Heracles asked, his voice edged with a trace of anger.

“Forgive me,” Melite replied, her tone soft and apologetic. “I was worried. I came to change your bandages, but then I saw you leaving the village and heading into the forest.” She added a hesitant gesture, as if bracing for his reaction.

Heracles’ gaze dropped to her frightened expression—and only then did he realize he was still gripping his sword, poised for a strike.

“It’s fine. You’ve done nothing wrong,” he said, his tone softening as he slid his sword back into its scabbard. “I’m grateful for your concern, but you don’t need to worry about me. I can handle myself—and you’ve already done more for me than anyone else ever would.”

“For a moment, I thought you might not recognize me before it was too late,” Melite replied, offering a wide smile, though her voice carried a faint tremor. “It was never my intention to unsettle you. I was just worried.”

Heracles’ eyes lingered on her, noting the quiver in her voice beneath the smile. That sliver of fear had not yet left her, and it stirred something within him he could not ignore.

“Why?” he asked, his voice low.

"Why what?" she replied, her brows knitting in confusion.

"Why do you care so much? I am a stranger to you—and you know what I truly am," he said, his tone edged with both curiosity and weariness.

"Can you not tell why?" she asked, her gaze locking with his, eyes searching his as though the answer should have been obvious.

Heracles said nothing. He had forgotten what it felt like to have someone care for him—especially in this way. It had been a very long time since anyone had looked at him like that. With his mind so consumed by his quest, he had not even realized how much he missed this feeling.

"Did you find what you were looking for?" she asked, stepping closer.

"No, I did not," he replied.

"Is that a good or a bad thing?"

"Both, I think."

"Are you done with this place?"

"Yes. I think I am."

"Would you walk me back to the village?" she asked, taking another step toward him.

"It would be my honor," Heracles said, a faint smile softening his expression.

Melite stepped closer and gently took his hand. "Come, I know a shortcut," she said, her voice soft yet certain. He followed without a word.

They walked in silence, the night enveloping them in its hush. He could feel her pulse through her hand—quick and steady. Despite the cold air, her small, delicate hand was pleasantly warm against his calloused grip. Before long, he realized they were not heading back to Dion. The path angled west, away from the village. Melite led the way with steady, purposeful strides, and though he understood where this might lead, he chose not to question her. Trust was not something he gave easily, but tonight, it came naturally.

The night was quiet, save for the soft crunch of leaves beneath their feet, but something in the air felt different. Glancing at her briefly, Heracles noted the resolve in her eyes but said nothing.

They arrived at a small cave entrance, tucked among the trees not far from the village. Melite stopped and turned to face him. "This is the place. I'm sure you'll like it," she said, her voice carrying a hint of excitement as she gestured toward the opening. He did not object; curiosity had already taken hold, and he followed her inside.

As Heracles stepped into the cave, a wave of warm, humid air greeted him, drifting from deeper within. The damp walls and ceiling glistened faintly in the dim light, and the change in temperature was immediate. His instincts had been correct—it was a hot spring. A natural pool of rock lay nestled in the chamber, its surface steaming gently. The vapor filled the small space, cloaking it in an ethereal mist that seemed to blur the boundary between reality and dream.

"What do you think?" Melite asked as she approached the pool and dipped her fingers into the water. "It's perfect," she said, not waiting for him to respond. Without hesitation, she began to undress.

Heracles stood motionless, captivated by the slow grace of her movements. Her long, straight chestnut hair cascaded over pale, youthful skin, the rich color accentuating her delicate beauty. As she slid off her tunic, her nearly flawless form was revealed—save for a small birthmark on her waist, a subtle imperfection shaped like an 'H.'

"What are you waiting for?" Melite asked as she slipped gracefully into the steaming pool.

He hesitated, the instinct to withdraw clashing with the quiet allure of the moment. He had long forgotten what it felt like to let his guard down—even briefly.

But this could be the last good memory he would ever have. Every step on this path he had chosen could be his last.

He unbuckled his belt, letting it fall to the ground before quickly shedding the rest of his clothes. Stepping into the water, he felt its warmth embrace his weary body. For a man so accustomed to battle and hardship, the moment felt strangely foreign—a brief reprieve from the weight of his quest.

Melite turned toward him, her gaze locking onto his, the intensity of it holding him in place. The night was fleeting, and she had no desire to waste another moment. With her heart pounding, she leaned closer, her lips brushing his ear, her voice low and intimate as she shared her secret—a truth meant only for him.

CHAPTER FOUR

THE PRICE OF PASSAGE

With Dion only a few hours behind, they began their descent down the final slope of Olympus toward the modest port below. Prometheus appeared as rested as his condition allowed, no longer leaning on Heracles' constant support to remain upright. Yet his pace remained painstakingly slow, each step deliberate. It was evident that the last of the golden apples of the Hesperides, miraculous as they were, had done little to restore him—after all, he was a Titan, likely the oldest living being in the Known World, burdened now by the weight of his endless years.

Heracles carried all the equipment alone, meticulously packed and wrapped to conceal the unfitting armor and weapons within. Such items were bound to draw unwanted attention, their divine craftsmanship unmistakable—a treasure beyond measure for any mortal fortunate enough to claim them. He hoped these extraordinary relics would suffice to secure passage to Colchis, confident they could persuade even the most obstinate captain to brave the perilous route.

As they reached the quiet port, Heracles observed a single ship moored alongside a few small boats bobbing nearby. If fate willed it, this ship might serve their purpose—provided the captain could be persuaded to sail them to their destination.

The few fishermen scattered around, engrossed in their daily tasks, paid no attention as Heracles and Prometheus stepped onto the dock. Heracles' gaze settled on a man near the dock's end, his attire noticeably more refined than that of those around him.

"Good day," Heracles said, addressing the man. "Are you the captain of this vessel?"

"Indeed, I am," the man replied, shifting his attention from a deckhand to Heracles.

"We would like to secure passage."

"But of course! Where are you headed? No, do not tell me, let me guess. Athens? No, Rhodes. No, no, that is not it. Aha, I have got it—Knossos, right?" the captain said, his tone brimming with enthusiasm.

"Colchis," he replied, cutting the captain's excitement short.

"Colchis?" The captain's demeanor shifted abruptly, his voice lowering. "A perilous journey, my friend—not one to take lightly."

"So, will you?" Heracles asked, his voice firm with conviction.

"Well, it depends. Normally, I would not—the Sea of Helle is a sight I seldom pass up. But it has been some time since I last sailed to Colchis." The captain's eyes sparkled with renewed excitement. "Perhaps I could be persuaded to err on the less cautious side."

Heracles unburdened himself, lowering their possessions from his back onto the creaking wooden dock. He opened one of the larger knapsacks and carefully removed the wrapped armor, setting it down with a heavy thud at the captain's feet.

The captain, unimpressed at first, began to study the armor as the sunlight caught its surface, revealing its exquisite details and unmatched craftsmanship. "Yes, this will do, my friend—this will do just fine," he said, his gaze fixed unwaveringly on the treasure before him.

"I'm glad. When are we sailing out?" he asked, hoisting the rest of their belongings onto his back once more.

"Soon, soon, my friend. Make my humble ship feel like home," the captain said. "You can take the cabin—rest. I will inform you when we depart, as soon as I have made the final arrangements for our journey." He offered a broad grin, his tone as cordial as ever.

As the day wore on, Heracles sat waiting in the small cabin of the ship, reminiscing about the previous night while eating some boar that Melite had tucked into their belongings. Those few hours, when his thoughts had been fixed singularly on one thing—her—were exactly what he had needed to fortify his resolve for the journey ahead.

"Why Colchis? Am I pronouncing it right?" Prometheus asked weakly, his voice drifting from the corner of the room.

"You are," Heracles replied, his mouth full. "Colchis is the furthest we can go from here. Besides, I've got some friends waiting there who might be able to help."

Prometheus did not respond to his answer; instead, he heaved a heavy sigh.

"You've got a friend there as well," Heracles added.

"I doubt it," Prometheus replied, his voice tinged with weary skepticism.

"Ladon would disagree," Heracles said, his tone laced with playful irony.

"Ladon?" Prometheus' face lit up—at least, as much as it could, given his broken features. "So, he is still alive after all these years? Praise Uranus! Is he well?"

For a fleeting moment, the weight of Prometheus' endless years seemed to lift. The thought of his old companion, still alive despite the centuries, stirred a long-dormant hope within him.

"Well, physically, yes. Mentally... I couldn't say," Heracles replied thoughtfully.

"What do you mean?" Prometheus asked, his tone shifting to concern.

"He's imprisoned inside the mountain—the same place where he slumbered for ages. He attacked Colchis after his cave was discovered, and I had to stop him. It's a long story. I'll explain everything along the way, if you wish."

"Fine. Knowing he is alive is enough for now," Prometheus said, settling back into his corner.

Heracles considered asking him a few questions, but before he could decide if the timing was right, he felt the ship lurch into motion. No one had informed them of the impending departure. Rising to his feet, he reached for the door, but it refused to yield under his touch—it was locked from the outside. He pushed gently, testing it, but it held firm. An alarm rang like a bell in his mind. This door had not been locked before and had no reason to be locked now. Something was wrong, and he already suspected the reason.

"Get up. We need to move," Heracles said as he approached Prometheus and grabbed his sword. "Something strange is going on," he added, his eyes scanning the cabin.

Stepping to one of the walls, he ran his fingers along the musty pine wood, feeling for a weak spot. "This will do," he muttered, before raising his sword and hacking into the wall.

Prometheus remained motionless, still bewildered by the sudden turn of events and Heracles' reaction. A loud knock on the door drew his attention, but Heracles did not seem to notice, continuing to hack away at the wall. Another knock, louder than before, failed to distract him.

"You there, can you hear me?" a voice called from outside. It was the captain. "What in Tartarus are you doing in there?" he asked, but made no move to unlock the door.

"Our departure was sooner than expected, and I apologize for not notifying you. We'll be making a brief stop at the island of Lemnos before continuing our journey. In case you are wondering, the door is locked for your protection—nothing more," the captain said, his tone measured, as though he had rehearsed it.

Heracles did not reply, nor did he pause; he had already carved a small hole in the wall.

Prometheus remained frozen, his mind racing to piece together the chaos unfolding around him.

"Prometheus!" Heracles called out loudly. "It's time to move. Grab everything you can and be ready—this won't take long," he added, continuing to widen the opening.

"I thought we could avoid this, but it seems we will not," the captain finally said from outside, his tone sharp as the fake mask of courtesy slipped away. "Fine, have it your way. Remove the bar."

Heracles clenched his jaw, frustration flickering in his emerald eyes. He had expected treachery but cursed himself for trusting the man, even briefly. There was no time for regret now—only action.

By the time they began removing the bar, he had already widened the hole enough for a person to pass through.

"Hurry up—knapsacks first, then you. Don't worry, I'll be right behind you," Heracles said as the door behind them swung open.

"By Poseidon, what have you done to my ship?" the captain exclaimed, his gaze fixed on the damaged hull. "I hope the price you'll fetch is worth all this trouble," he added, signaling to his crew.

In unison, the crew rushed into the cabin, swords drawn, the glint of bloodlust sharpening their eyes. But Heracles was ready. The first man in line slammed face-first into Heracles' calloused fist, the impact sending him reeling. Without pause, Heracles deflected the incoming attacks, his movements precise and unrelenting.

Prometheus, now grasping what was happening, scrambled to throw the knapsacks through the opening, his hurried movements going unnoticed amidst the chaos as Heracles kept the crew at bay.

Though outnumbered, the cabin's cramped quarters worked in Heracles' favor, forcing the attackers into single-file assaults he could repel with ease. He deflected another strike and slashed across the attacker's throat in a single motion.

The man collapsed, gurgling as blood flooded his airway, his life ebbing within moments. The rest of the crew hesitated, frozen by the sight—until the captain's furious shouts drove them forward again.

Heracles saw that the death of one crewmate would not stop the rest. He could kill them all—easily, even. But that was not the answer. These were slavers, true, but slaughtering them would make him no better than the monsters he fought. There had to be another way. Without a second thought, he expertly disarmed the nearest of them, striking him hard with the lion-head pommel of his sword. Grabbing the stunned man, he hurled him with force into the others, creating just enough space to slam the door shut in their faces. Quickly, he dragged a heavy oak cabinet from nearby and braced it against the door, hoping it would hold them back long enough for their escape.

Prometheus had just thrown the last knapsack through the opening when Heracles appeared behind him.

"Let's go. I hope you can swim," he said, grabbing Prometheus before leaping off the ship.

They hit the sea with a loud splash, plunging beneath the surface from the force of the impact.

The water was warm, and the bright sunlight danced across the ripples above. Heracles found brief solace in the muffled silence beneath the water, allowing himself to relax—but only for a moment.

Prometheus' frantic struggle to resurface snapped Heracles back to the present. He surged through the water without hesitation, gripping Prometheus tightly as he guided him upwards. When they broke through the surface, Prometheus gasped for air, clutching Heracles' arm for support. Relief flashed across his exhausted features, though he managed a faint nod of gratitude.

He glanced at Prometheus, his weakened state evident in the way he struggled to stay afloat. "Can you manage on your own? The shore isn't far," he asked, his voice steady, though his gaze betrayed a flicker of concern.

"I will," Prometheus replied, though his voice lacked conviction.

After a few moments of swimming, they reached the shore, the ship still visible in the distance. Heracles paused for a moment, the saltwater stinging his eyes as he scanned the horizon. The weight of the soaked belongings dragged at his arms, but the soft sand underfoot offered a fleeting sense of safety. He let his body collapse onto the warm, golden grains, allowing himself to catch his breath.

Prometheus, utterly exhausted, lay face down at the water's edge, the gentle waves lapping over him.

"Guess we're walking," Heracles muttered, rolling onto his back with a weary sigh. "No rest for the cursed."

CHAPTER FIVE
THE PREDATOR'S SNARE

After several uneventful days of walking, they arrived at the outskirts of Methone, a northeastern coastal village nestled where the lands of Pieria and Emathia converged. The settlement, perched along the rugged coastline, served as both a fortress and a harbor—its strategic position guarding the united kingdoms under King Pierus' rule.

Methone was not merely a stronghold but the lifeblood of King Pierus' naval power. Pirates and marauders alike dreaded its name, for the Emathian navy was famed for its unmatched prowess at sea, led by his two daughters, Achelois and Tritone. Celebrated for their sharp intellect, striking beauty, and voices so enchanting they could rival the Muses themselves, the sisters inspired both loyalty and awe among their crews.

Farther along the dirt road, a carriage sat motionless in a rut where the path dipped sharply, the low ground pooling rainwater and turning the soil into a thick mire. As Heracles approached, he noticed the carriage's wheels sunk deep into the clinging mud. The driver—his face flushed with frustration—was furiously striking the flanks of the struggling donkeys with a weathered stick, his curses shattering the stillness of the surrounding fields.

"Come on, you stubborn beasts, move!" the driver bellowed, lashing the poor creatures with unrestrained fury.

Prometheus, having quickened his pace over the past day, walked close behind as Heracles stepped forward.

"By Apollo! Where did you two come from?" the driver exclaimed, visibly startled. "You scared the life out of me!"

"Stuck?" Heracles asked.

"Obviously," the driver replied, oblivious to the sarcasm as he sized Heracles up with a scrutinizing gaze. "You look like you can handle yourself, though I can't say the same for your companion. How about giving me a hand? These damned beasts won't listen to no one."

"Grab the donkeys' reins and pull," Heracles instructed as he strode to the back of the carriage.

Before the driver could even tug at the reins, the carriage jolted forward, its wheels breaking free from the clinging mud with a wet squelch.

“Great, stop—this will do,” the driver exclaimed with enthusiasm, releasing the reins abruptly and narrowing his eyes at the donkeys, his expression filled with barely concealed disdain.

“I owe you one, big man,” he said with a nod of gratitude as he climbed back onto his seat atop the carriage.

“How about a ride to the outskirts of the town?” Heracles asked, his tone casual.

“Jump in,” the driver replied, punctuating his words with a welcoming wave of his hand.

Heracles hefted their belongings onto the carriage and helped Prometheus climb aboard before settling into the back himself. The wooden frame groaned in protest under his weight, the sound echoing faintly in the still air.

“Move it, you useless beasts,” the driver barked, tugging sharply at the reins.

The donkeys obeyed, slowly pulling the carriage forward. The ride was a welcome change after the long trek from the small port of Dion. To their relief, the weather had improved—clear skies now replaced the black clouds and driving rain of the previous day, which had battered them for hours.

Prometheus seemed to revel in the rain, hardly pausing his stride throughout its duration. When he did stop, it was only to lift his face to the sky, letting the droplets crash against his skin. Heracles did not question him; in truth, he occasionally mimicked the gesture—though with far less enthusiasm than Prometheus seemed to feel.

The fortifications of Methone were now clearly visible in the distance. Heracles was not certain that visiting the town was a wise decision. A place like this—teeming with guards and watchmen—offered little besides idle gossip and far too many prying eyes for his liking. Even cloaked, he was taller and broader than most, and his eyes were a dead giveaway to anyone paying even a moment's attention.

The outskirts will do just fine for now, Heracles thought, striking the wooden frame with his knuckles to signal the driver to stop.

"Just leave us here," he said, motioning for Prometheus to rise.

"As you wish," the driver replied, tugging the reins sharply to bring the carriage to a halt.

The driver waited for them to disembark, offering a brief gesture of farewell before urging the donkeys onward. Heracles and Prometheus stood watching the carriage recede into the distance until Heracles pointed toward a structure that might serve them for the night. It appeared to be an old mill—or perhaps a watchtower—likely abandoned this far from town.

The place was indeed vacant, its upper structure largely destroyed. As they approached, Heracles thought a roof would have been a welcome addition, but as long as the weather held, it would suffice. At the very least, it offered some semblance of shelter until morning. They did their best to make the space as comfortable as possible amidst the rubble—clearing a bit of ground and dragging over a couple of large stones, just broad and flat enough to sit on. Heracles kindled a fire to stave off the chill settling in. Their provisions were running low, worsened by Prometheus' appetite, which had begun to return—albeit slowly.

"I think I'll hunt for a while. I should be back before dark, but if for some reason I'm late, don't come looking for me. I'll be fine. Stay here," Heracles said firmly.

Prometheus, seated with his cloak draped over him, covering everything but his face, seemed utterly entranced by the flickering flames of the fire.

"Prometheus!" Heracles called louder, snapping him out of his trance. "Did you hear a word I said?"

"I will stay here until your return," Prometheus said, his voice devoid of emotion, then resumed his vacant stare at the fire.

Heracles exhaled through his nose and gave a slight shake of his head—a gesture of quiet resignation—before gathering his gear: the bow, the quiver, a length of rope, and a goatskin of water. His sword remained ever at his side, as it always had. As he turned to leave, he glanced back at Prometheus, who remained oblivious to his departure, still fixated on the dancing flames.

As darkness began to overtake the fading light, Heracles' irritation deepened. He had found nothing worth hunting—not even a rabbit. By now, he would have gladly shot a squirrel, had one been unfortunate enough to cross his path.

Something moved at the edge of his vision—a shadow, large and shifting. Heracles crouched, holding his breath, and waited for it to reveal itself. He could not see it yet; the dense vegetation obscured its form. A sudden rustle in the underbrush followed, and a deer emerged. It was not as large as the shadow had made it seem, but it would be more than enough to call this a successful hunt.

Heracles nocked an arrow with measured precision, raising the bow with slow intent. He drew the cord back smoothly, his movements synchronized with a deep, steady breath. His aim settled on the deer's flank, trained on its heart. But before he could release the shot, a sharp noise from farther off startled the animal, and it bolted in a blur of motion.

Heracles cursed under his breath and moved toward the sound. He soon reached a clearing that offered an unobstructed view of the town, only then realizing how far he had strayed. Beneath one of the scattered trees dotting the landscape, he caught movement, though the encroaching darkness blurred the details. The muffled sounds, however, were unmistakable—someone was screaming.

Without hesitation, he rushed toward the source of the commotion, his suspicion confirmed as the scene came into focus. What he had not anticipated was the sheer brutality of it: a young woman was fighting with all her strength, struggling desperately as a man held her down.

"Stop!" Heracles shouted, his voice booming as he slowed from a sprint.

"By Apollo, it is you again. Your timing is as perfect as ever," the man sneered, striking the woman hard across the face.

"Stand still—this just got more interesting," he added with a wide grin, revealing the few teeth he had left.

Heracles felt a surge of disgust. That voice—he knew it. The same man who had given them a ride not long ago.

"I said stop," Heracles repeated, his voice low as he halted just a few feet away.

"Why stop? Why not join me?" the man jeered, his grin widening. "I am sure this bitch would gladly keep us entertained for a couple of hours." He struck her again—this time even harder. "What do you say, big man? Fancy going first? I do not mind watching to get in the mood."

The woman, frozen in fear, tried to scream once more, but before she could even part her lips, the man's hand tightened around her neck, cutting off her breath as he raised his other hand.

Before he could carry out his intent, Heracles seized his arm and wrenched him away from her.

"What are you doing, you big moron? Let me go, or I'll—" The words died in his throat as Heracles struck him across the mouth with such force that his lips split open.

As the man tried to rise, Heracles struck him again, further reducing his teeth to single digits.

Though the urge to do more burned within him, Heracles held back, delivering a single, punishing blow with his knee to the man's diaphragm.

The impact drove the air from his lungs, leaving him curled in agony on the ground.

Heracles slowly approached the woman, who had retreated to the base of the tree, sitting with her knees drawn to her chest, her arms wrapped tightly around them in fear.

"It is over. Are you hurt?" he asked gently, concern evident in his tone as he offered her some water from his goatskin.

The woman shook her head, remaining silent.

"Are you from the nearby town? Do you live close by?" he continued.

This time, she nodded, taking a small sip of water.

"Do you need help getting back?" he asked.

"No. What about him?" she asked, her voice trembling.

"Do you know him?" Heracles inquired.

"I do. He is the local gravedigger. Bastard!" she spat, glaring in his direction.

"Can you handle a bow?" Heracles asked, extending his hand to her.

The woman hesitated at first, but when she met Heracles' eyes, she saw kindness within them, despite their unusual appearance.

She extended her hand and, with his assistance, rose to her feet.

Heracles placed the bow in her hands before turning his attention to the man, who was still curled on the ground, struggling to catch his breath.

"I am restraining myself from breaking your legs, so I suggest you stay down," Heracles warned the man.

He then turned to the woman. "If he even tries to get up, shoot him. I'll just need a moment."

Heracles approached the tree and uncoiled the rope slung across his chest. He had not expected to use it for anything other than tying his prey, but things rarely went as planned.

He moved to a smaller tree nearby and, with effortless strength, chopped it down. From the fallen trunk, he cut a piece just the right length for his purpose.

Returning to the larger tree, he secured one end of the rope to the bark and tossed the other over a sturdy branch, fashioning a noose.

After testing its weight, he placed the log beneath the noose and turned to retrieve the man, who was still sprawled on the ground, breathing heavily.

Grabbing him by the foot, Heracles dragged him toward the tree, ignoring the muffled protests spilling from the man's bloodied mouth.

With ease, he hoisted him onto the log, bound his hands behind him, then tightened the noose around his neck.

Heracles cast him a final look, scorn etched across his face.

Leaving the man there, mumbling and begging as blood dripped from his lips, he turned back to the young woman, who stood rooted in place, stunned by the sudden turn of events.

"I will leave the rest to you," Heracles said, giving her a small nod.

She nodded back, then handed the bow back to him. But before he could leave, she reached out and grasped his hand.

“I have nothing to offer you but my gratitude,” the woman said, her voice trembling as a tear rolled down her cheek.

“That is enough. Take care,” he said, his voice steady.

Without another word, he turned and walked into the darkness, leaving the choice to her alone.

CHAPTER SIX

OF MONSTERS AND MEN

The morning sun climbed steadily as Heracles and Prometheus made their way toward the lively market of Methone. The guards at the city gate, though silent, cast more than a few curious glances their way.

Though Heracles wished to avoid risky detours or delays, sustenance was a necessity. The market's winding rows were brimming with provisions—everything they needed for the journey ahead.

Heracles never spoke of the previous night to Prometheus, nor did Prometheus ask. For Heracles, such horrors were all too familiar; he had witnessed the darkness men harbored in their hearts. Beyond the safety of towns and cities, acts of murder, rape, and other savageries were all too common—far too common for his taste.

Monsters, he could understand. They were non-sentient, driven by survival—no morals, no hatred, no true evil. But mortals? They had the power of choice, and that was the breaking point. He could not fathom why mortals chose evil, yet he punished such choices relentlessly, no matter the cost. Still, he tried to offer every creature a chance, even when the world made such efforts feel futile.

"Prometheus," Heracles said, indicating a shop. "Stay close."

Prometheus nodded and followed as Heracles stepped inside.

"Good day, travelers," the shopkeeper greeted them, turning to face them. He wiped the blood from his hands on the apron stretched over his ample belly. "What brings you to my store?"

"Well met," Heracles said. "Anything fresh will do."

"My friend, everything here is fresh. We've got boar, deer, pheasant—or even chicken, if that suits you." The butcher's eyes glinted with pride. "In fact, I slaughtered a fat, juicy pig just this morning. It'll make an excellent roast. What say you?"

Before Heracles could answer, the butcher set to work, chopping the pig into smaller pieces.

"It'll do. I'll take all the finest cuts."

"Really, all of them? Now that's a proper customer! I already like you, my friend," the butcher said, his enthusiasm sharpening his movements as he chopped with renewed vigor.

Heracles glanced at Prometheus' weary face. "Do you know of a good place that serves refreshments?" he asked.

"But of course! The tavern closest to the dock—you can't miss it."

"I'm grateful. I'll return for the meat," Heracles said, exiting the store. "Let's have a drink while we wait. It'll be some time before we reach the next town."

Prometheus did not reply. He simply followed closely, as instructed.

They reached the dock, and as the butcher promised, the tavern stood nearby, lively with patrons.

They settled at an empty table closest to the water.

Several ships were moored along the quay, smaller fishing boats bobbing between them. Most of the vessels were built for war, the shields affixed to their railings making their purpose unmistakable.

A guard came running toward the tavern, his face flushed from the sprint. He hurried to a table crowded with soldiers, collapsed onto a bench, seized a kylix brimming with wine, and drained it in a single motion.

"I need volunteers for a hunting party," the guard said, wiping his mouth with his arm. "A gryps has been sighted to the north." He reached for another kylix.

"What in Tartarus is a gryps?" another soldier asked, bewildered.

"It's a griffin, you half-wit. A huge, eagle-like lion monster. Believe me—if you'd ever seen one, you'd remember it," the red-faced guard said, taking a long gulp of wine.

"Sounds like your wife," another soldier quipped, and the table erupted in laughter.

Heracles had seen a griffin only once, from a distance, long ago on his way to Colchis. These creatures rarely attacked mortals, as they lived on the fringes of the Known World, usually keeping to the mountains. Some even claimed they were drawn to gold and often guarded areas rich with such deposits.

There was no evidence to support these claims, though—no one with half a brain would dare confront such a monster, especially on its own territory.

Within the hour, Heracles drank his fill, purchased provisions with the last of his gold, and, with Prometheus by his side, headed out of Methone toward the north.

They continued along the main road for a while before reaching a large ranch not far from the path. As they passed, Heracles noticed a paddock where several horses grazed—the sight suggested this was likely a place where horses were bred and sold.

He considered visiting the ranch to acquire a horse, but he had no gold left. He could offer something from his gear in trade, but the bow and shield were invaluable for their journey, whereas a horse would only ease their travel. Still, there was no reason not to speak with the owner; perhaps they could come to some sort of arrangement.

As they approached the place, an old but well-built man emerged from the main building and walked toward them.

"Greetings, good travelers! What brings you here?" the man said warmly.

"Well met. Are these horses for sale?" Heracles asked.

"Indeed, they are. Interested? Which one caught your eye?"

"The cheapest will do just fine."

"Ah, I see. I can let that brown one go for some gold or silver—no gems, though," the man said, shaking his head.

"Is there something I can do to help in exchange for the horse?" Heracles asked.

"Unfortunately, no. We don't need any more hands," the man said, his expression apologetic.

Heracles clenched his jaw, reluctant even to ask. "Trade?"

"Sure, I can trade—depends on what you offer."

Heracles dropped their belongings to the ground and began to unwrap the shield. Before he could finish, a faint screech sounded in the distance.

"By Poseidon, what was that?" the old man exclaimed, glancing around in fear.

Heracles already knew what it was and began unwrapping his bow instead of the shield.

"I think you should hide. You too, Prometheus. Get inside the house and stay there." He looked at the old man. "Is there anyone else around here?" he asked calmly.

"No, it's just me and my daughter. The rest went to town for the night. What was that? Do you know?" he asked, teetering between fear and panic.

"I think I do. It doesn't matter—move," Heracles said, his serious look underscoring the urgency of the situation.

Without argument, they both hurried inside the house, leaving Heracles behind.

He strapped on his quiver just as a louder screech split the air. Gripping his bow, he took cover behind a stone well.

Above the tall trees beyond the ranch, a massive figure burst forth, wings beating furiously as it hurtled toward the field. Its golden eagle head gleamed in the sunlight, eyes like molten amber fixed on its prey. Feathers gave way to the muscular body of a lion, its talons curved and gleaming like razors. The sheer force of its descent sent a ripple through the air as it crashed down atop an unlucky horse, crushing it with a sickening crunch of bone and flesh.

Its leonine muscles rippled beneath a coat of tawny fur, while its wings, lined with deep ochre feathers, spread wide.

A high-pitched shriek tore through the air, making Heracles' ears pop.

As the griffin began tearing into the warm flesh of the horse, Heracles nocked an arrow but did not release it. He hesitated, uncertain whether to engage the creature. So far, it seemed focused solely on feeding, and letting it finish its meal might be the wisest course of action.

However, before he could decide, a group of soldiers rushed toward the griffin, shouting and cursing, weapons in hand.

The griffin seemed oblivious to the shouts, continuing to devour its prey. A volley of arrows flew, some finding their mark and interrupting its feast. It raised its head, blood dripping from its beak, and spread its wings wide.

A piercing shriek tore through the air—a bone-chilling blend of an eagle's cry and a lion's roar. The griffin's blood-slick beak snapped open and shut, a silent threat, its feathered chest heaving with primal fury.

The soldiers froze in place, clutching their ears in pain.

Yet the griffin did not attack. It simply stood there, waiting.

"Run, you fools," Heracles murmured, still in cover.

But they did not. Instead, they formed a semicircle and began advancing toward the griffin.

Heracles, realizing there was no other choice, rushed toward the soldiers just as the monster launched its lethal assault.

The griffin lunged. The first soldier did not even scream—its talons cleaved him nearly in half.

The creature continued its onslaught, slashing at soldiers with its talons and sending them flying yards away. One soldier tried to hurl a spear, but the griffin's wing slammed into him, the force shattering his bones as he collapsed to the ground like a snapped branch.

Finally within range, Heracles loosed an arrow that struck the griffin mere inches below its wing. The impact staggered the beast, and it unleashed a guttural screech.

As it struggled to tear the arrow free with its beak, Heracles seized the opportunity and fired a second shot, this time piercing its neck.

The griffin shrieked in agony. Without hesitation, Heracles tossed his bow aside and drew his sword. He sprinted forward and leapt at the beast, grabbing onto its feathers tightly.

It thrashed and bucked, but he clung on with relentless determination.

With a sudden surge, the griffin spread its wings and attempted to take flight. Heracles climbed onto its back and slashed at the base of its wing. A torrent of blood gushed from the wound as the griffin crashed to the ground.

Crimson soaked its ochre feathers as Heracles leapt clear, rolling gracefully as he landed.

The few remaining soldiers, seeing the creature injured and vulnerable, rushed to attack.

"Stop!" Heracles shouted. "Enough—the beast is done!"

But the soldiers did not listen. Before they could close in, the griffin staggered to its feet. Despite its limp, bleeding wing, it managed to lift off and retreat—its flight unsteady—as it fled in the direction it had come.

"By Poseidon, what was that thing?" one of the soldiers said, staring at the griffin as it slowly faded into the distance.

"Shut it. Go check on the others," another soldier ordered, stepping toward Heracles. "You there—we're grateful for your help. Stick around; our superiors would like to express their gratitude as well."

"I was just passing by," Heracles said. "May your fallen find peace." He nodded respectfully toward the soldier.

"We were fortunate you were here," the soldier replied, returning Heracles' nod.

"I'll be on my way." Heracles turned toward the ranch house.

"Are you sure you can't stay? The captains would reward you well."

"I'm sure. Farewell," he said, and began walking to the house. He had no time to waste, nor any desire for reward. He had simply done what was right.

Inside, silence greeted him. He moved from room to room—each one empty, save for a single door, shut tight. He tried the handle, but it was locked. Knocking gently, he waited patiently until he heard the sound of a bolt sliding open.

The door opened to reveal the old man, worry etched deeply into his face. Behind him, Prometheus sat quietly in the corner. Beside him, a young woman lay on the bed, turned away from Heracles.

"It was you, wasn't it? She told me only of a large man with strange eyes who came to her rescue. That's you—no doubt this is more than coincidence," the old man said, staring at him.

"You saved my daughter, and now you've saved me as well. How could I ever repay you?" he asked, his voice thick with emotion. “Take any horse you want—no charge. It’s the least I can do.”

With his arms barely reaching around Heracles, he hugged him as tightly as he could.

CHAPTER SEVEN
A DEBT OF BLOOD

Several days had gone by since they left the outskirts of Methone and passed the small town of Aigai. They barely exchanged a word.

Heracles had accepted the old man's original suggestion and taken the cheapest horse—brown, seasoned, and strong—despite the man's repeated offers of his finest steed.

Prometheus, seated sideways on the horse's back, seemed to enjoy the ride in silence. Whether out of respect, contemplation, or something else entirely, Heracles could not say. As they neared Pella, he chose to hold off on initiating conversation.

After the long ride, Heracles thought a brief rest near Pella would be prudent—it might also give Prometheus a chance to finally speak. Though he had left the matter to the Titan, Heracles was beginning to suspect that Prometheus might never speak at all.

So far, the journey had been pleasant, with no incidents or surprises—the road mostly empty, save for the occasional merchant passing by.

"We'll make a stop soon. Are you doing well?" Heracles asked, ruffling the horse's long brown mane.

"I am fine," Prometheus responded.

Heracles did not press him, urging the horse to pick up its pace instead.

After a few more uneventful hours, they reached the outskirts of Pella. The town was renowned for its lush forests and natural springs—an ancient haven where nymphs were said to dwell, their blessings or curses shaping the land's fate.

This was not the first time Heracles passed through the area, and he knew it well—its forests, its history, and the men who ruled it. In places like this, knowing who held power could mean the difference between peace and conflict.

Though Pella technically belonged to the kingdom of Emathia and Pieria, it had its own ruler: King Karanos. Renowned for his imposing stature and peerless combat skill, Karanos had earned his position through valor. King Pierus, recognizing his strength, granted him authority as a subordinate king under his banner, entrusting him with command of the ground forces in times of war. Together, the two kings forged a formidable alliance—one built on the rare and potent combination of elite infantry and a powerful navy.

Heracles pulled the reins, bringing the horse to a halt as he surveyed the area. The outskirts were mostly flat, with tall trees forming a natural barrier that obscured the view beyond. As the sun sank low on the horizon, he guided the horse off the main road and toward a nearby forest. The animal let out a soft whinny but followed Heracles' lead into the greenery without resistance.

They moved through the untamed forest, Heracles ducking beneath low-hanging branches until they emerged at a small, serene lake. He brought the horse to a stop and dismounted with practiced ease. Approaching the water's edge, he knelt and scooped some into his palm, drinking deeply. The cool, crisp taste was invigorating, stirring faint memories of Thebes—his distant home.

It had been far too long since he had last set foot in Thebes—longer than he cared to admit. The town was small but strikingly beautiful, with two large, glimmering lakes nestled beyond its northern edge. He recalled his mother, Alcmene, leading him to one of them as a boy, where she would occasionally bathe him. She had a rare gift for making him laugh until his sides ached and he could scarcely breathe. Those moments remained among his fondest memories.

Alcmene was not only a loving mother but also a remarkably clever queen; few could match her wit—including his father, Amphitryon.

Shaking the memory loose with a quiet breath, Heracles stood and turned back to the horse.

"Come on, Prometheus. We'll stay here for the night," he said, unloading their belongings from the steed.

Prometheus dismounted slowly, lowered his hood, and drew a deep breath.

"I can smell their presence on the air," he said, eyes closed. "Almost taste it."

"What do you mean?" Heracles asked, not pausing as he worked to make camp.

"The Muses. Their scent—is familiar. Reminds me of something I have long forgotten."

"And how exactly does familiar smell?"

"Faintly sweet. Like a song I once knew but can no longer name."

"Great," Heracles said, without pausing. "Stay here. I'll be back soon," his mind already turning to the tasks ahead as he strode off to gather firewood.

Once Heracles had disappeared into the trees, Prometheus took the horse's reins and led it slowly to a nearby tree, tying it securely before walking toward the lake. He waded into the water until it covered his feet. Lifting his tunic, he inspected the wound on his chest. It looked better—not healed, but clearly improved. He placed a hand over the wound, closed his eyes, and listened. But he heard nothing. Nothing at all.

As the half-moon's light shimmered on the lake, Heracles sparked the wood to life and sat across from Prometheus. Reaching for a nearby knapsack, he drew out an amphora of wine and took a deep swig. His gaze shifted to Prometheus, who once again seemed entranced by the fire. Yet something about him had changed. His eyes, once entirely white, now held a more pronounced shade of blue. In his long white hair and beard, a faint tint of red had begun to emerge. And if Heracles had to swear it, Prometheus seemed just a little taller.

"You are staring," Prometheus said quietly, his head still lowered.

"Do you want some wine?" Heracles asked, awkwardly offering the amphora.

"Tell me about Ladon," Prometheus said, accepting it.

"As I told you already, he is fine—alive, but confined to his cave. I needed to find the Garden of the Hesperides, and he helped me. The only thing he asked in return was an audience with you."

"And you said he is in Colchis? Is it far?"

"Yes, and yes. But we have a horse now—this will speed things up," Heracles said, grabbing a piece of meat. "Is it true you fought alongside him?" he asked, setting the meat on a rock beside the fire.

"The dragons joined us in the war, sealing their fate," Prometheus said, sighing softly.

Heracles paused, watching Prometheus carefully. "So, you really know nothing of this world, do you?"

"It looks the same, but it feels different."

"Do you know how long it's been?"

"Does it matter?"

"No. You're right. It doesn't. At least not anymore," Heracles said, taking back the wine.

After a moment of silence, broken only by the faint sizzle of roasting meat on the stone, Prometheus lifted his head.

"Tell me—what is your end goal?" he asked.

"To right the wrong," Heracles said bluntly.

"Why? This world looks fine—not perfect, but far from burning," Prometheus said with a heavy sigh.

"It's true, the gods don't care much anymore, but that doesn't absolve them of the countless lives lost to their cruelty. Look at what they did to you! Don't you want to fight back? I thought you wanted revenge!" Heracles said, his voice rising—burning hotter than the fire itself.

"Look at me. What can I do? I owe you my freedom, and I will do whatever you ask of me. But in the end, I am a mere old man," Prometheus said, lowering his head.

"I promise I'll find a way to remove your curse. All I need from you is your trust—the rest will follow," Heracles said, and Prometheus nodded.

"Good. Now eat. We still have a long way to go," Heracles added, offering the meat to him.

The night passed quietly, broken only by the crackling of the fire and the occasional rustle of leaves, as they both slept peacefully.

A loud noise jolted Heracles awake in the dead of night. Rubbing the sleep from his eyes, he froze as a second sound—louder this time—echoed from behind him. Grabbing a stick of wood from the still-burning fire, he rose to his feet.

As he moved toward the source, the grisly sounds of flesh tearing and skin ripping filled the air, making his skin crawl. He thrust the makeshift torch toward the noise, its flickering light revealing a gruesome sight: the horse being devoured by the griffin.

He drew his sword, the metallic scrape of the blade against the scabbard halting the griffin's feast. It raised its massive, feathered head—blood dripping from its beak—and locked its piercing gaze on him.

"You accursed beast! Damn you! You've taken what little we had. Every step forward drags us two steps back—and now you're here, feasting on my only damn horse! Was this some kind of revenge?" Heracles roared, his voice booming like a tempest.

"It wasn't my damned fault! The soldiers were fools—worthless fools—but even they must follow orders. I had no cursed choice!" He stood ready to strike, his eyes ablaze with fury.

The griffin remained motionless, its piercing eagle eyes still fixed on him.

“Fine. Gods-damned fine. I suppose we’re even now. Take your meal and begone,” Heracles growled, his voice low as he gestured for it to leave.

The griffin spread its massive wings, sank its claws into the flesh of the dead horse, and took to the sky.

A drop of blood struck Heracles’ face—a grim reminder that fate is fickle, and that justice or vengeance never comes without blood.

CHAPTER EIGHT

THE WEIGHT OF THE HEAVENS

High above the clouds, the peak of Mytikas stood untouched by mortals, its summit piercing the sky nearly ten thousand feet above the ground. Frozen and immutable, it marked the highest point in the Known World—a threshold between heaven and earth, as scholars whispered in awe.

At the edge of the peak, a figure draped in black stood unmoving, their gaze fixed on the distant horizon.

Heavy snowflakes collided with their face—a countenance both ancient and ageless—vanishing the instant they touched.

A sharp cry pierced the storm as a massive eagle burst through the tempest, its feathers catching a faint metallic sheen in the swirling snow. As it descended toward the figure, the air seemed to ripple in its wake, stirred by unseen currents. The figure extended an arm in silent invitation, and the eagle landed with precision, its talons gripping firmly as its powerful wings beat once before folding close.

"What didst thou see, mine old friend? Speak now, for the winds whisper of change," the figure intoned, their voice calm yet commanding, as the eagle shrieked sharply.

"I see. Very well—keep both thine eyes upon them," they commanded, raising their arm to release the eagle to flight.

The figure took a deep breath, exhaling slowly before turning to descend from the peak. With each step, the divine aura of the summit seemed to fade, yielding to the quieter majesty of the mountains below. The snow lay deep, rising nearly to their waist, yet it did not hinder their steps in the slightest.

As the snow thinned along the figure's descent, they reached a small threshold guarded by two sentries.

"My King!" the sentries declared, dropping to their knees in unison before him.

He pressed onward, reaching a vantage point that offered an unobstructed view of the Plateau of the Muses. From this height, the grandeur of divine creation unfolded: the city of Pantheon sprawled across the plateau, its structures shimmering like prisms beneath the interplay of sunlight and snow—a masterpiece untouched by mortal flaw.

With regal steps, he entered the city. Every sentry he passed knelt in reverence, their heads bowed before their king. He made his way toward the grand palace at the far end of the city, which rose above all else, commanding the heights.

The gates parted as he approached, and he stepped into the palace without pause. The architecture within revealed its splendor—marble seamlessly intertwined with gold and silver, a fusion of stone and metal that defied mortal comprehension. Such craftsmanship was, to the gods, a natural expression of beauty—unbound by earthly constraint.

The King entered the grand hall of the palace, where the divine seat of power rose at the far end. Upon the marble throne, adorned with intricate metallic designs, sat a young man in a relaxed posture.

"Good morn, Father," the man greeted with an easy air.

"Where is she, Hermes?" the King asked as he came to a stop before the throne.

"She is still with Mother. Her wound has proven quite... severe," Hermes replied.

"Did she say anything else?"

"Other than the fact that she fought and lost to a demigod? No, I do not think so," Hermes said, crossing his legs with deliberate ease.

"Summon Pandora," the King commanded, his voice resounding with conviction.

"Why? Allow me, and I shall see it done swiftly," Hermes replied, a wry smile curling his lips.

The King fixed Hermes with a searing stare, his eyes a vivid, otherworldly blue, flickering with a faint spark. That single glance sent Hermes jolting off the throne, stepping aside to vacate the seat.

"I could..." he began, but the King's thundering voice cut him off.

"Now, Hermes," the King commanded, striding toward the throne.

Before he could turn to sit upon it, Hermes had already vanished in the blink of an eye.

Zeus exhaled heavily, his shoulders sagging slightly as he placed a hand to his forehead. The weight of his thoughts pressed down on him like the very heavens he ruled—vast, cold, and eternal.

CHAPTER NINE
CHAINS OF THE PAST

A few miles from the town of Pella, in the heart of the small, placid lake, Heracles floated effortlessly on his back, his body perfectly still as the water held him aloft. The crisp chill of the lake lingered, but the bright morning sun tempered it, casting a gentle warmth across his skin.

With his ears submerged, Heracles muted the clamor of the world around him—a quietude he had cherished since childhood. The muffled hum of the water offered a rare serenity, soothing his restless thoughts and granting him a fleeting escape from the weight he carried.

Prometheus sat at the lake's edge, his feet barely skimming the water's surface. His fingers traced the scar on his chest in slow, deliberate strokes, following the jagged line from top to bottom—again and again.

It had been a fortnight—perhaps longer—since their escape from the prison of Olympus, yet he still struggled to believe he was truly free. A part of him remained bound, as though the chains endured, and the shadow of his torment had never lifted.

It was he who had persuaded Heracles to stay here for a few days. This lake was the first place where Prometheus felt a sense of familiarity in a world that otherwise seemed strange and unwelcoming. Seeing him at ease for the first time, Heracles had agreed without hesitation or protest.

"Are you hungry?" Heracles shouted, but Prometheus did not respond.

Heracles began to swim slowly toward the shore and, upon reaching Prometheus, playfully splashed water at him, jolting him from his thoughts.

"Did your daydreaming give you an appetite? Because my swim certainly did. You like fish? I'm pretty sure I saw some carp out there," Heracles said.

"I do," Prometheus responded, a speck of excitement in his tone.

"Great! Looks like today's activity is fishing," Heracles declared as he walked out of the lake. "Come—we'll need to make a couple of spears."

At their small encampment, Prometheus sat on the ground near the firepit, where a faint warmth still lingered. Heracles dressed and secured the sword at his waist.

"Where did you find that sword?" Prometheus inquired in a low voice.

"As far as I know, it was a gift," Heracles responded.

"From whom?"

"From my father—my real father," he said without emotion, though his fist tightened around the sword's grip.

"You mean Zeus," Prometheus countered, his tone tinged with resentment.

"Yes. Are you ready to talk?"

"What do you want to know?" Prometheus replied, lifting his head.

"Let's start with that wound on your chest. Does it hurt?" Heracles asked, his voice laced with both curiosity and concern.

But before Prometheus could respond, Heracles was overcome by a sudden and intense sensation.

Before the hairs on his neck could even rise, a young man appeared out of nowhere—mere yards away—standing motionless in the middle of the forest.

Heracles instinctively drew his sword, locking his gaze on the stranger.

“Easy there,” the young man said, sunlight glinting off the silver-coated plates of his armor.

Though lightly built, the armor’s craftsmanship was exquisite, with gold engravings decorating most of its surface. But what caught Heracles’ attention most was the man’s helmet—resting above his luscious blonde curls and strikingly handsome visage, it bore two wings, one on each side.

Recognizing who he was, Heracles took a quick glance at Prometheus, who remained seated; his expression did not betray surprise, but rather concern, as Heracles quickly refocused on Hermes.

“Before you ask—no, you cannot have him,” Heracles said with his usual conviction.

“Have him? Pray, I am not here for him. That antiquated relic means nothing. I am here for you, bastard!” Hermes replied, his grin brimming with anticipation.

“Are you sure you want to do this?” Heracles asked, his voice weighted with a heavy heart.

Hermes smiled wide and, with a fluid motion, unsheathed his divine short swords in a graceful flourish. As Heracles shifted into a defensive stance, Hermes burst forward with such speed that Heracles barely managed to block the attack. Their blades clashed and locked just before his face—the edge of Hermes' sword grazing his chin and leaving a shallow wound.

"At last, we meet face to face," Hermes said playfully, his dark blue eyes gleaming with radiant white—spreading outward like rays of the sun, alight with excitement.

Heracles pushed Hermes back, breaking the lock of their swords, and moved in to attack. Hermes parried the strike with ease, turning his wrist slightly to redirect the blow. Unfazed, Heracles struck again, delivering a powerful vertical blow with both hands. But Hermes effortlessly twisted his body sideways, letting the blade pass harmlessly by.

Heracles followed up with a horizontal swing aimed at Hermes' upper body, but Hermes leaned sharply backward, his torso arching like a bow in midair. For a moment, he seemed weightless—his balance unbroken—as he planted his swords into the ground behind him. Using them as supports, he let Heracles' blade pass mere inches from his chest, a calm smile playing on his lips.

The last swing threw Heracles off balance, and Hermes gracefully straightened before delivering a sharp kick to his back, sending him tumbling to the ground.

Hermes then turned his attention to Prometheus, who still sat by the firepit. This time, however, his expression had darkened—turning almost bitter.

"Is he your salvation? Honestly? I expected more. Either Artemis is out of shape, or she has grown soft fawning over her precious beasts," Hermes said with a short laugh.

Before Prometheus could reply, Heracles' fist struck the ground as he slowly pushed himself back to his feet.

"Ready for the next round?" Hermes asked, still looking at Prometheus.

"Spare me the talk," Heracles replied, steadying himself for the fight.

Hermes' attack came so fast that Heracles barely managed to deflect it—but not before the blade sliced into his shoulder. The next strike followed from Hermes' off-hand sword, and though Heracles shifted his footing in anticipation, the blade still cut deep into his thigh.

Paying no attention to his wounds, Heracles retaliated with a wide horizontal slash, which Hermes parried with one blade—Olympian metal grinding against Olympian metal. In a seamless motion, he brought his second sword across, trapping Heracles' weapon between both blades like a vise. With a sharp twist and pull, he tried to wrench the sword from Heracles' grasp—but he had underestimated his strength.

Heracles' arms braced, veins pulsing beneath taut skin as he planted his feet. His teeth clenched, and a low growl rumbled from his chest. A single beat of silence passed—heavy with the strain of locked weapons.

Then, Heracles yanked the sword toward himself, pulling Hermes close enough for his left fist to crash into the god's youthful, perfectly aligned face.

Hermes absorbed the full force of the blow, staggering as he tried to retreat. But Heracles pressed the attack relentlessly. Still dazed, Hermes struggled to block the incoming strikes as Heracles put his full weight behind each swing.

Every blow drove Hermes back until his spine struck a tree—just as Artemis' had before him.

"I don't want to strike you down," Heracles said, pausing his attack.

Hermes tilted his head, intrigued. "Why not?"

"Because I don't have to," Heracles admitted, lowering his sword.

Hermes could see the sincerity in him—no wrath, no hatred, only resolve in those green eyes, so much like his own, yet undeniably different.

"Enjoy your freedom while you still can," Hermes declared—and in a blur of motion, he launched into a flurry of strikes.

Once again caught by surprise, Heracles tried to parry, but Hermes' movements were too fast—every blow found its mark. One swing cut deeply into Heracles' sword arm, just above the wrist, weakening his grip—just enough for the next strike to disarm him.

With a swift pivot, Hermes moved to Heracles' side and slashed his leg just above the knee. Following through with a spinning strike, he cut across Heracles' back, sending him crashing to his knees.

Blood poured from his wounds, darkening his tunic as a small crimson puddle quickly formed beneath his leg—the flow so heavy the earth could not absorb it fast enough.

"Your honor is your undoing," Hermes said, stepping in front of him.

Heracles slowly raised his head and smiled at him—Hermes had trapped his neck between both blades.

"Moral choices are not made for the sake of their consequences," Heracles intoned, turning his gaze to Prometheus. "They are made because one holds them to be just."

He could see the sadness on Prometheus' face, laced with bitterness—darker than before.

"Pray forgive me," Prometheus said, his voice heavy with regret.

Still smiling, Heracles blinked slowly at Prometheus, then closed his eyes and took a deep breath.

"Not so fast," Hermes said, pulling his swords away from Heracles' neck and striking him hard at the temple with a pommel.

Heracles collapsed, his eyelids fluttering as he fought to stay conscious—until darkness overtook him.

Hermes approached Prometheus and crouched before him.

"Well, old man, you see the futility now, do you not? Your legend is forgotten and will never be heard again. You have no power, and no one will save you. I wish I could end this now, as it should have ended a millennium ago—but alas, I cannot.

"Perhaps someday. But not today."

Prometheus closed his eyes for a moment—and when he opened them, Hermes was already gone. He stared into the emptiness left behind, his jaw tightening as resentment welled within him.

CHAPTER TEN
THE SILENT BURDEN

The day was nearing its end, and from the palace balcony, the sun could be seen slowly—yet steadily—sinking behind the mountain peak, casting a long shadow over the city of Pantheon.

It was a grand city, not as vast as Colchis or Athens, yet its beauty was beyond compare. More striking than its splendor, however, was the unwavering devotion of its people—every resident blindly loyal to the King, prepared to obey his every command.

Not all who dwelled within the city were gods, but each bore the mark of divinity. Many were of semi-divine nature, freed from the frailties of mortal existence.

Zeus, leaning against the marble railing of the balcony, gazed upon the city, worry etched into his face. The breeze stirred his long white hair and beard, the silken strands shifting like drifting clouds beneath the golden daylight.

With a slow breath, he cast his concerns aside and turned, stepping into the palace interior.

At the center of the chamber, a woman of exquisite beauty sat in silence before a table cluttered with objects and tools crafted for the arcane and alchemical arts. Her black hair, streaked with white, was woven into an intricate braid that cascaded to her waist.

“Is she here?” Zeus asked as he sat beside her.

“She will be here very soon,” Hera replied, watching him closely, her eyes a deep, rich brown, encircled by thin rings of gold that gleamed subtly in the light. “Are you certain about this?”

“Do you have a better proposal?” he said with a sigh.

“What if I do? Would it matter?” She arched a brow. “It did not matter then—why would it now?”

“How is Artemis?” Zeus asked, attempting to steer the conversation away.

Hera did not answer immediately. Instead, she continued to stare, as though still waiting for a response of her own. At last, she said, “She is fine—nothing serious.”

Zeus nodded absently, his mind adrift, until a knock at the door pulled him from his thoughts. “Enter.”

The door eased open, admitting a slender woman draped in a flowing white chiton, its fine fabric cinched at the waist with a delicate gold cord. Her long golden hair cascaded down her back, catching the light with a soft shimmer as she stepped into the room.

"My King, my Queen," she said, bowing with effortless grace.

"Pandora, welcome. Sit with us," Hera said.

"I require something of you," Zeus said as Pandora settled into her seat.

"Your will is mine to fulfill," she replied with a sincere smile.

"You must find Prometheus and bring him to me," Zeus said, his tone unwavering.

"Of course. Whatever you wish—but may I ask, why me?" she inquired.

"Because I trust no one else. I want him alive." He gave the final word deliberate weight.

"It shall be done, my King," she said, inclining her head in deference.

Zeus rose to his feet. Out of respect, Pandora inclined her head as he nodded and strode from the room. She moved to follow, but before she could, Hera caught her by the wrist.

With Zeus gone, Hera gestured for Pandora to accompany her to the farthest corner of the chamber, where a cabinet stood. Pandora followed without hesitation as Hera opened it and retrieved a plain sword—unadorned, its hilt devoid of embellishments, the blade bearing no engravings or divine markings. It was no different from the weapon of a common mortal soldier.

"Take it," Hera said, offering her the sword.

"My Queen?" Pandora's sweet visage faltered, confusion flickering across her features.

"Prometheus is accompanied by a dangerous man. Use this sword to kill him—and Prometheus," Hera said, her gaze piercing.

In that moment, every trace of sweetness vanished from Pandora's face, dissolving in instants. What remained was sorrow—deep and bitter.

"Since your parents fell in the Titanomachy, I have cared for you as one of my own and taught you everything I know. You are a sorceress beyond equal. Trust me—it must be done," Hera said, pressing the sword into Pandora's hands.

"What of the King?" she asked, the weight of the blade settling on her like a burden too heavy to bear.

"Do not trouble yourself over him. His mind is clouded by emotion. Prometheus is a threat to us all. And as for his companion—it was he who unchained the Titan, and he must answer for his actions. Now take it and go, child," Hera said, gently brushing Pandora's hair behind her ear. "Do not falter. You are doing what must be done."

Pandora tightened her grip around the sword's hilt. It had not grown heavier, yet it felt heavier all the same. She drew a slow breath, steadying herself, forcing away the doubt that crept in.

She bowed her head and turned toward the door, her movements deliberate, measured. The cold metal pressed against her palm—a silent burden she could not yet name.

Her orders were clear. No matter what she felt, fate had set her on this path.

CHAPTER ELEVEN
BENEATH THE STORM

The sky was dark, heavy clouds blotting out the stars as rain hammered down, drowning the sound of Prometheus' ragged breathing and the scrape of Heracles' body being dragged across the wet ground.

Hours had passed since Prometheus, with difficulty, had placed Heracles on a fur hide along with their belongings and begun the long, arduous journey toward Mount Pierus.

He had no logical reason for heading there—only a feeling. A quiet pull in his chest, a flicker of instinct that spoke of safety, perhaps even aid. He could not explain it, but he trusted it nonetheless.

Their progress was painfully slow, even with the ground still flat beneath them. Heracles' weight was considerable, and Prometheus' weakened state made the task all the more grueling. Yet he had no choice—Hermes had seen to that.

Every so often, Prometheus stopped to check on Heracles. Most of the wounds had stopped bleeding, save for the one in his foot, where the bandage remained soaked in blood. His color had drained, leaving his face and body deathly pale, and his breathing was shallow—barely perceptible.

The sky flared with jagged lightning, slashing unevenly across the darkness like a dull sword. A near-deafening clap of thunder followed, driving Prometheus to his knees as exhaustion overtook him.

He lifted his face and let the raindrops crash against his skin—a reminder of the punishment he no longer had to endure. A thousand years of captivity and torture was more than any being could withstand, but he had survived—though not without losing a part of his former self. That loss terrified him, a fear he hid from Heracles—and from himself.

"No," he said, his voice heavy. With a loud grunt, he forced himself to his feet. "You will not die this day."

With the mountain in sight, Prometheus pressed on through the downpour that had soaked everything around him. Every step was a triumph, even if each one was slow as a snail's crawl. His strength was nearly spent—his arms burned with pain, and his feet felt as though they might break.

The fog veiling the mountain peak was thick, almost otherworldly, curling around the stone as though shielding it from unwelcome eyes.

Though Mount Pierus was not especially tall, its distinction lay in the dense vegetation that blanketed nearly every part of it. Under the rain, it shimmered with a ghostly silver sheen—as if a faint shaft of moonlight had slipped through a gap in the clouds, illuminating the glistening leaves.

Now, nearly at the slope, Prometheus' foot slipped on a rock, sending him sprawling onto the wet ground with a dull thud.

The wind stirred the grass, grazing his weathered face and gently caressing his skin—like a mother soothing her child to sleep. The brief respite took him, and unconsciousness followed.

Klymene had always been a gentle and caring woman, never wishing harm upon anyone—even when the gods took up arms against them, even when one of her beloved sons fell in the fray after accepting the quest to infiltrate Mount Olympus and steal the divine fire for mortals. Not even when her spouse, Iapetos, died horribly in battle at the hands of Ares, son of Zeus and Hera.

She loved her children more than anything—each of the four equally and without distinction.

Yet she shared a unique bond with one of them: Prometheus, the eldest of her sons.

The day of his birth, just as he emerged from her, time seemed to stop. Everyone felt it—but for her, it was stronger, more profound. At the time, it had meant nothing. But as the years passed, she came to understand that Prometheus was different from the rest of the Titans.

His mind was not bound by their vast, yet divine, limitations. It was clear he could see beyond the threshold—and even if she did not fully understand it, she was proud of him.

Especially because, despite his extraordinary mind, Prometheus possessed a pure, benevolent heart—a rare trait among gifted deities.

The last day he saw her was before her end—the day he and his brother Epimetheus left for Olympus. She held him tightly in her arms, stroking his soft red hair, which curled slightly at the ends and glinted like burnished metal touched by flame in the morning light.

Her hand lingered at the crown of his head as she whispered in his ear, "I love you, son, and I am proud of the man you have become. Watch over your little brother—and remember, lead with your mind, but fight with the strength of your heart."

“Mother!” Prometheus gasped, trying to open his eyes.

“Rise, Titan,” said the figure above him, her tone warm as she caressed his long white hair. “Come with us.”

Prometheus’ eyelids fluttered, and through his blurred vision, he saw a woman dressed in white lingering above him. Her scent was familiar, and her touch and voice were soothing. He tried to rise, but before he could manage it, his strength failed him—and darkness swallowed him once more.

A feeling of weightlessness overtook him, like being carried by the wind. He blinked through the blur, catching flashes of Heracles being borne effortlessly in the arms of another woman beside him, his limbs swaying in time with her steps.

“Do not worry, all will be well. Rest now,” the first woman whispered softly as she carried Prometheus in her embrace.

For a moment, he felt safe, as though the heavy burden had been lifted—and he succumbed to sleep.

When he opened his eyes again, he was somewhere else—somewhere the rain could not reach. It was an enormous cave, and every inch of its walls was covered in vibrant flora. A myriad of flowers—krokos, galanthos, fritillaria, ramonda, and krikon—adorned the stone, their colors bleeding into one another in bursts of red, white, and deep violet.

The scent was overwhelmingly strong, like Mount Hymettus in the spring, where the fragrance of thyme, honey, and wildflowers could carry for miles.

"Welcome, Prometheus. It has been a while," said the tall woman standing nearby. Her visage was like a sculpture of masterful detail, wrought to perfection. Her pale skin accentuated her delicate features—long auburn hair flowing over her shoulders, and deep hazel eyes brimming with wisdom.

"Come, follow me," she said, smiling with heartfelt kindness as she extended her hand toward him.

Prometheus accepted her offer and took her hand gently. She pulled him to his feet with effortless grace, and as he rose, the familiar sweet scent washed over him again, stirring a distant memory.

"Calliope!" he gasped, the memory of her surging to the surface.

"You remember. Good. Come along—you probably want to check on your companion," she said, leading him by the hand.

They reached a chamber where Heracles lay on a stone bed, encircled by three women kneeling with their eyes closed, all dressed in white. Their robes draped over their slender frames, pooling at their feet like mist.

Their intricate braids of light auburn hair were woven with ivy, dark green leaves curling through the strands like living thread. Delicate white flowers peeked between the braids, their petals catching the low light with a soft gleam.

Each one was distinct, yet they all shared the same delicate features—high cheekbones, narrow brows, and serene expressions untouched by time.

They hummed a melody that transcended the very space around them, the sound light and pure, like distant chimes carried on the wind.

However, Prometheus' face was etched with worry at the sight of Heracles' bare, wounded body. Deep cuts marred his skin, the bruises already dark and swollen beneath pale flesh. Dried blood clung to his knuckles, the faint metallic tang sharp in the cool air. His breath was shallow, rattling faintly with each slow rise and fall of his chest.

"He will be fine. My sisters will take good care of him—he just needs time to heal. Come, I wish to converse for a while," said Calliope as she turned and walked out of the chamber.

It was now clear to Prometheus who these women were—the Muses, divine sisters of inspiration, creativity, and knowledge. Calliope was the eldest of the nine, and the three around Heracles were Clio, Euterpe, and Polyhymnia.

Clio's posture was poised and dignified. Euterpe's delicate hands moved slightly in time with the melody. Polyhymnia's serene expression was untouched by strain. Heracles was in good hands—and if anyone could save him now, it was them.

"Pray, this way," said Calliope, gesturing for him to follow.

She led him to an opening in the cave that resembled a natural stone balcony, overlooking the distant sea. The storm had passed, and godrays pierced the clouds, spilling golden light from the hidden sun. A rainbow arced across the sky, its vibrant colors crowning the landscape.

"You must be famished. Help yourself," she said, offering him a seat beside a table filled with fresh fruits and vegetables.

Prometheus settled onto the seat and took a large, ripe fig. He could not recall the last time he had tasted something so sweet, and for a fleeting moment, he felt a spark of joy.

"How did you escape?" Calliope asked, pulling Prometheus back to reality.

"With his help," Prometheus answered.

"You understand what that means?"

"I do."

"Good. What happened?"

"Hermes."

"I see. Strange that he did not kill you both."

"I do not know. Probably because Zeus wants me back in my chains."

"Naturally. Do you have a plan?"

"We do. We are heading to Colcis."

"You mean Colchis. Yes. The distance may serve you well." Calliope's gaze drifted toward his chest. "His hold is still strong on you. May I?"

Prometheus nodded and lifted his tunic, revealing the scar. She slowly reached out, placed her hand on his chest, and closed her eyes.

Her lips parted in a soft, murmured incantation as her eyes moved rapidly beneath her lids. He felt a warm current surge from the center of his chest, washing over his body and momentarily freeing him from fear and doubt. Even after her hand lifted, the feeling of safety lingered.

"This will have to do for now. Forgive me—that is all I can do. The curse is still potent," she said, lowering her eyes as if unable to face him.

"I feel better. You have my gratitude. What about Heracles? Do you think he will be fine?"

"Do not worry about him. He is extraordinary—stronger than anyone we have ever healed. He will be a good protector for you. His heart is still pure."

"What do you mean by 'still'?" Prometheus asked, furrowing his brow.

"The influence of the gods has no root in him, but your path will be fraught with divine conflict—as it already has. He is a demigod, after all, and Olympian blood flows through his veins. Do not let him be corrupted, because without him, I fear you do not stand a chance—especially in your condition," Calliope said, looking Prometheus straight in the eyes.

Prometheus nodded in understanding with a heavy sigh as Calliope leaned in and caressed his hair, her touch light and deliberate.

"Trust your instincts, as you always have, Titan," she said, her voice low and sure.

She turned and left him gazing into the distance, where Olympus still loomed faintly—its jagged peaks cutting through the thinning clouds like the edge of a blade.

CHAPTER TWELVE

A VEIL OF CLOUD AND SONG

Heracles opened his eyes and lurched upright, only for a sharp pain to arrest his movement before he could stand. He groaned, grinding his teeth as he tried to make sense of his surroundings.

Through blurred vision, he spotted a familiar figure seated in the corner of the room, a heavy tome resting in his hands.

“Prometheus? Is that you?” Heracles asked, struggling to sit upright on the bed.

“Yes. Take it slow. We are safe here,” Prometheus replied, closing the tome.

“Where are we? What happened?” Heracles asked with a heavy groan.

“We are on Mount Pierus, in the sanctuary of the Muses. They tended to your wounds. How do you feel?”

“I feel as though I’ve been trampled by a cavalry charge,” he muttered, rubbing his eyes. “Wait… did you say Muses?” he added, his voice tinged with disbelief.

"Indeed. We have been their guests for several days now," Prometheus answered, moving closer. "Would you like to meet them?" he asked, offering his hand.

Heracles took it and slowly rose to his feet. As he stood before Prometheus, he blinked—and froze. There was life in his eyes—a spark of clarity, vivid and unmistakable. The dull whiteness was gone, replaced by the full brilliance of divine blue. He looked younger now, stronger, and streaks of red had begun to overtake the white in his hair and beard.

"You look better... or do my eyes deceive me?" Heracles asked.

"Probably. Though still better than you," Prometheus replied with a faint smile.

"Good. That means you're carrying our belongings now," Heracles countered with a slight nod.

"Come. Let us go see them."

Heracles leaned on him for support as they walked slowly through the lush vegetation of the cave, until they reached a chamber that resembled a dining hall, where the three sisters were seated.

They approached the table, and Prometheus helped Heracles ease into one of the chairs—its base carved from stone, its seat smoothed with wood.

“Greetings, Heracles,” said Clio in her soft voice. “Are you feeling better?”

Heracles, momentarily entranced by their beauty, took a breath before answering.

“I think so. Prometheus said you helped me. I am truly grateful—and glad to repay the favor, if I can.”

“We are happy to offer our aid to someone such as you,” replied Euterpe with a warm smile.

“A friend of Prometheus is a friend of ours,” Polyhymnia added. “You must be hungry. Pray, help yourself.”

The table before them was laden with vegetables and fruit, and a modest serving of meat—scant in quantity, yet somehow enough for even Heracles.

“We do not feast on meat,” said a calm voice as Calliope entered the chamber and took her seat, “but we thought you might enjoy it.”

“Heracles, it is my honor to introduce you to Calliope,” Prometheus said with quiet respect.

Very few things could draw Heracles’ attention away from food—but in that moment, it no longer existed to him. Calliope’s visage was breathtaking.

Though her features resembled those of her sisters, there was something singular about her—an aura that made her presence irresistible, mesmerizing.

"The honor is mine," Calliope replied, her features aglow like the sun. "Pray, feast. You need the nourishment."

Heracles bowed his head and, without further delay, began to eat—in his usual manner, grabbing handfuls of food and swallowing without chewing, letting out guttural sounds of pleasure.

Calliope and her sisters exchanged glances, snorting in amusement and disbelief as they watched him devour everything before him, cleaning each plate with single-minded zeal. They tried to hide their smiles as best they could, though their eyes betrayed them.

Later that day, on the stone balcony of the cave, Prometheus and Calliope stood in silence, gazing out at the horizon. Olympus was no longer visible; a thick fog had rolled in, cloaking the world below in a pale, shifting veil of cloud.

The air was still—heavy with moisture—as though the mountain itself were holding its breath.

“I think it is time to leave,” Prometheus said, breathing anxiously.

“You may stay longer, if it pleases you. You are safe here,” Calliope replied in her calm voice.

“I know. But you have done more than enough already. I would not bring trouble to your doorstep.”

“As you wish. Know that you will always be welcome here,” she said, meeting his gaze—those unmistakable eyes, cerulean threaded with faint sparks of red, like embers buried beneath still water.

“I could not be more grateful. I swear, one day I shall repay the favor,” he said, bowing low before her.

The next morning, they gathered their belongings—along with supplies generously provided by the Muses—and made their way to the cave’s entrance to offer their farewells.

“I meant to ask—where are the others?” Prometheus inquired.

“Euterpe and Urania have gone to Delphi. The rest are on pilgrimage. I am sure they will be saddened to have missed you, but they will be overjoyed to hear that you are free and well,”

Calliope said, stepping forward and drawing him into her embrace.

Heracles took his turn, placing a hand over his chest and bowing before them as deeply as his injuries would allow. Calliope stepped toward him and placed her hands on his shoulders. She leaned in and whispered into his ear:

"We need men like you, Heracles. For when none dare to stand for what is right—that is when the monsters rise. Not from darkness, but from silence."

Her words struck like a creed, resonating deep within his soul, as though her voice had reached inside and touched it.

She leaned back, and Heracles nodded in understanding—even if he could not fully grasp the depth of her words.

With Mount Pierus behind them, they made their way east, toward the Strymon River and Amphipolis—leaving behind silence, song, and something unspoken.

CHAPTER THIRTEEN

EYES IN THE CANOPY

After several days of travel across the flat, open landscape of Emathia, the borders of Thrace came into view at last. Dense forests clung to the slopes of steep mountains lining the frontier, their looming presence rendering the passage both treacherous and largely undesirable.

Most travelers preferred the coastal path, which—though significantly longer—was far easier to traverse. From the east, the route passed through Amphipolis, skirted Stagira, and curved inland above the peninsulas of Athos, Sithonia, and Pallene, before finally reaching Pella.

Another route began near Lake Strymonida, where travelers boarded boats and drifted downstream along the Strymon River, arriving at the harbor of Amphipolis. From there, they could continue by ship in any direction, while those on foot followed the coastal path southward.

Heracles and Prometheus, however, were approaching from the west, and since they wished to avoid major cities, they chose to pass through the wilderness instead.

Heracles knew the path would likely be less safe, but they had already spent several days in respite, and Prometheus was in better condition than before—still far from the ideal travel companion, yet moving with noticeably greater ease. Taken together, these reasons made the quicker route worth the risk.

Heracles inquired about Prometheus' renewed strength and appearance. He still resembled an old man, but no longer appeared quite so rugged or stiff. He no longer hunched forward, nor did his steps remain heavy and dragging. His hair and beard had grown healthier, with strands of red returning, and the deep wrinkles in his skin had begun to fade. He had even taken to carrying some of their belongings, as Heracles was still recovering.

Most of Heracles' wounds had already healed, save for the one in his leg. Though it still caused him some pain, his condition had greatly improved. The injury continued to hinder him slightly, yet he remained in far better shape than Prometheus. What surprised him most was that many of his older scars had nearly faded away.

"Good," Prometheus had said the day before, as they bathed in a cold stream. "Now you have space for more."

It was the first time Heracles had heard him attempt a joke, and truth be told, he rather liked it. He had to admit his body was beginning to look more scar tissue than skin.

Later that evening, they reached the edge of the forest and chose to rest before venturing deeper into the wild.

The Muses had provided them with an abundance of supplies, and Heracles wasted none of it. Each time he took a bite, his thoughts drifted to Calliope's final words—and the way she had spoken them. He felt a connection—not the same bond Prometheus shared with them, perhaps, but a strong one nonetheless. Calliope reminded him of his mother—not in appearance, but in spirit. He had needed that push more than he had realized. And though still battered by injury, he felt stronger now—more certain, less burdened.

As Heracles drifted into sleep, his thoughts wandered again—to the distant kingdom of Colchis, and above all, to Medea and Podargos. It had been many months since he had last seen them, and he longed to be reunited with them. He harbored no worry for the colt—Podargos was in good hands.

Medea, though—his final glimpse of her, pale and trembling outside the protective barrier of the Draconian Gate, lingered in his mind. He could not shake that image of her. He had never seen her so weak, and that unsettled him. Yet if there was ever a woman who could endure anything, it was her. Of that, he had no doubt.

As the sun rose, bathing the world in a reddish-gold glow, Heracles stirred from a light, restless sleep. He grabbed a few pieces of fruit from one of the knapsacks and ate as he stretched his limbs.

"Good morn. Care for some breakfast?" Heracles asked, exhaling with effort.

Prometheus sat up on his bedding and shook his head.

"I didn't sleep well. And you?" Heracles asked.

"I believe I had a dream, though I cannot recall it," Prometheus replied, scratching his beard.

"That's normal. I rarely remember mine," Heracles said as he continued stretching.

"I do not dream. I cannot even recall the last time I dreamt."

"Really? That's strange. Do you know why?"

"I think it is the curse—and likely no coincidence I dreamt after Calliope's help,"

Prometheus said, rubbing his face. "The wound is still here, but I feel lighter..."

"Less burdened," Heracles said, finishing the sentence.

"Exactly," Prometheus replied, turning his attention to Heracles, his expression softening.

"Well, like I said, I feel better. Are you ready? This path will slow us at every turn, but we'll gain at least a fortnight over the main road."

"I am ready when you are," Prometheus said, his gaze sharpening with focus.

The forest in this part of Thrace was the thickest and wildest of all. Only the woods beneath Mount Haemus came close, yet even they lacked such density. The trees loomed like ancient sentinels, their thick limbs interlocking high above to form a ceiling of shadow, allowing only a few stray rays of sunlight to squeeze through. Barbed bushes snarled across the forest floor—impenetrable and twisting—forcing them to push and struggle forward like prey caught in a hunter's snare.

Within this forest, even the air felt drained of strength. The place stood still, and the canopy hung so high that not even the rustling of leaves could be heard. Black pine trees dominated the woods, their towering forms blotting out the sky in layered walls of green. Their bark—gray to yellow-brown—split into wide, flaking fissures that formed scaly plates, deepening with age and revealing just how ancient these trees had become.

The silence was broken only now and then by the soft thud of pollen cones dropping onto thick grass and pine needles.

Their movements were slow, as it was impossible to walk in a straight line—though Heracles often chose to stomp straight through the bushes and brambles in their way. Prometheus simply followed the path Heracles carved with his immense build. Not once did he appear lost; at every stage of the journey, Heracles' sense of direction rivaled that of a seasoned hunter.

Thus, Prometheus never questioned him, following along with quiet trust.

After several hours of grueling travel, Heracles stopped and looked around.

"This wretched forest is getting on my nerves," he muttered with a groan.

"Are we stopping?" Prometheus asked.

"No, not yet. We must be close to the mountain range. We'll stop there and decide whether to climb or look for a pass. Let's push on for now," he said, taking a deep breath and moving forward.

A few hours later, they came upon scattered rocks—a sign that they were finally nearing the edge of the forest. Heracles had been right; in the distance, a slope now came into view. As they approached the base of the mountain, Heracles stopped once again and scanned the terrain ahead.

"Well, it looks steep. I don't think we can make the climb—but I've also had enough of this forest. We'd better look for an easier place to ascend, or see if there's a pass. Either way, I'm beat. We'll camp here for the night—unless you have any objections?" he said, waiting for a reply.

"I will go gather some firewood," Prometheus said, setting his burden down before heading off into the underbrush.

He did not have to go far—the forest was an endless source of fuel, and with no rain in days, every piece he gathered was dry and perfect for kindling.

As the sunlight slowly faded, Prometheus picked up the last piece of wood and turned back toward camp. A distant cry drew his attention, stopping him mid-step. He strained to make sense of it—then, from somewhere in the distance, a faint voice rose: "Help me."

“Who is there?” Prometheus shouted.

“Mercy,” came a haunting voice from another direction, echoing faintly through the dim forest.

“Where are you?” Prometheus called again, louder this time.

“Forgive me,” came another voice—closer now.

“Grant me peace,” came yet another—this one from behind him, just as haunting as the others.

Prometheus found himself surrounded by ghostly voices—pleading, begging, closing in from all directions. They crept nearer with every word, and though they sounded like genuine cries, there was something unnatural about them—something hollow beneath the sorrow.

Sensing the danger, he tossed the wood aside and ran as fast as he could back to camp. The voices stalked him, hunted him, urging him to stop and offer mercy, to grant them clemency and forgiveness. But he did not stop. Not until he reached Heracles.

“Do you have the firewood?” Heracles asked, still arranging stones around the already lit fire, his back turned to Prometheus.

“There is something wrong with this forest,” Prometheus said.

Heracles turned to face him, ready to agree on how much he loathed the place—only to find him panting, wide-eyed, and winded.

"Don't tell me gathering wood is that much of a chore," Heracles said.

However, before Prometheus could reply, a cry rose from deep within the forest, snapping Heracles' head toward the sound.

"What in Tartarus is going on?" he said, beginning to walk toward the voice—only for Prometheus to grab his arm and stop him.

Confusion flickered across Heracles' face as he looked at Prometheus—whose expression was etched with concern.

"What are you doing? We should help," Heracles said.

A faint stir of wind rippled through the high canopy, sending dry needles sifting down. Heracles stiffened. The shadows no longer felt empty.

But before Prometheus could reply, another voice crept from the forest.

"Aid me," came the ghastly call, sending a chill down Heracles' spine.

"Give me amity," echoed another voice—closer this time—and Heracles instinctively grabbed the hilt of his sword.

More voices rose from ahead, to the left, and to the right—but not from behind, where the mountain stood. Prometheus' gaze slid to Heracles' hand as he released his grip on his arm.

"Grab a stick of wood and use it as a torch," Heracles whispered, slowly drawing his sword. "These are no men's voices. They sound like... ornithes."

"What should we do?" Prometheus asked, grabbing a stick and plunging it into the fire.

"Survive," Heracles said, as the myriad echoes of unnatural voices suddenly ceased. "Get ready."

With the sun almost entirely hidden behind the canopy, a deep silence overtook the forest. Only Prometheus' heavy breathing and the crackling of the fire pierced the thick layer of stillness.

A small, shadowy figure emerged from a tall tree ahead and dove toward them—only to meet Heracles' sword head-on. Sparks flared at the point of impact as he deflected the strike, driving the shadow-black creature to the ground with a sharp shriek—one he silenced beneath the full weight of his boot, twisting and grinding his heel until the thing was crushed beneath it.

"What is it?" Prometheus whispered, angling the torch to better see the creature.

It resembled a crow, but something was wrong—its feathers were not feathers at all, but coarse, soot-black filaments that shimmered like oil. A short, ragged tail flared behind it, shaped like that of a taōs—better known as a peafowl—but tattered and uneven, as if scorched. Its beak curved like a stournos'—a starling's—but thicker, serrated near the base, and made of something that looked disturbingly like forged metal: dull, dark, and shaped like a flesh-harvesting scythe.

It was massive—but in the wrong way: too heavy, too dense, as if carved from bone and metal rather than grown. Unbalanced. A thing that should not fly, yet did. And it carried the stench of death itself—sweet rot, the acrid tang of rusted metal, and something fouler still: a sickly, sour reek, like spoiled milk left out beneath a corpse.

Heracles' boot remained planted on its twisted form, but even crushed, one talon twitched—just once—as though death had not fully claimed it.

He did not reply at first, his eyes scanning high into the trees, his stance poised for battle.

A cacophony of screeches filled the forest—shrill, grating, like jagged bone dragged across stone.

"Here they come," Heracles said, still not answering Prometheus' question, as he grabbed his bow and swiftly nocked an arrow.

An ornitha burst from the trees and pitched into a steep descent, but before it could reach them, Heracles fired—his arrow struck with a heavy thud, stopping the creature mid-flight and sending it crashing onto its back. Its legs kicked high and twitched violently—a final spasm of defiance.

Heracles kept firing as more ornithes descended upon them, each one falling to the sting of cold metal. But they kept coming, and soon, his quiver would be empty.

He wasted no arrows, hitting his mark with every release of the string. He nocked the final shaft, and just as he was about to let fly, an ornitha came at him with such speed that he nearly failed to dodge. Its beak caught his arm, slicing the flesh as it passed.

The creature beat its wings, trying to wheel around for another strike—only to meet the flame of Prometheus' torch. Its feathers caught fire like kindling. It flailed in panic, screeching, then crashed to the ground in a burning heap.

The next few moments were a frantic struggle to stay alive. The ornithes came in shrieking waves, wings thrashing and beaks flashing, but each charge was broken by fire and metal. Prometheus swung the torch in savage arcs, searing feathers and blistering flesh, while Heracles tore through them with his sword—hacking into bone, splitting sinew, cleaving wings from bodies. Blood sprayed in dark jets across the churned earth, and the air reeked of scorched meat and rot.

The ground was strewn with corpses, and the sharp tang of blood—mingled with a heavier, rotting stench—hung thick in the air.

Then, at last, as the final light bled into dusk, the attack ceased.

The forest fell still—eerily still. Not a cry, not a wingbeat. Whatever remained of the flock had vanished into the dark, leaving the two of them soaked in blood and sweat. Only the crackle of fire and the faint sound of their breathing filled the void where chaos had been.

Heracles held his stance a moment longer, eyes scanning the trees, sword raised and dripping.

Prometheus stood frozen, the torch gripped tight in his hand, its flame flickering as his fingers trembled.

The weight of silence pressed down like a held breath. Heracles remained taut—motionless, but ready—his focus unshaken. Prometheus stayed still, though his gaze slowly climbed toward the treetops.

A single black feather drifted from above and landed on Heracles' sword, clinging to the blood that coated most of the blade.

"Well," Heracles muttered, wiping the blade clean in the crook of his arm. "We were nearly butchered by a flock of damned birds."

CHAPTER FOURTEEN
WHERE NONE RETURN

Darkness veiled the forest—thick and stifling—as though the night itself sought to smother all life beneath its weight. The oppressive blackness was broken only by the dim flicker of the dying campfire, its glow casting long, quivering shadows across the undergrowth.

Heracles remained alert, crouched beside the blackened corpse of the first creature.

"They're called Ornithes—flesh-eating birds," he said at last, flicking the feather into the fire. "I've fought them before. Not like this."

Prometheus watched him. "And what changed?"

"Me, I think," Heracles said.

"What do you mean?" Prometheus pressed.

Heracles seemed to fall into deep thought for a moment, his expression shifting between confusion and realization, back and forth.

"I think I am responsible for these Ornithes being here. Like I said, I fought the Stymphalides back in my youth. It was a bounty from Eurystheus, the king of Tiryns and Mycenae. I was tasked with driving away a flock of deadly birds that had gathered around Lake Stymphalia in Arcadia—hence the name Stymphalides Ornithes.

"These birds were no ordinary creatures. They were man-eating, with metallic beaks and razor-sharp metal feathers. Some accounts even claim their droppings were poisonous. They dwelled in marshy terrain, which made it nearly impossible to fight them on foot.

"To solve this, I used krotala—clappers, like castanets, but forged from Olympian metal. I used them to startle the birds into flight. Once airborne, I brought many of them down with bow and poisoned arrows. The rest of the flock fled and were never seen in that region again."

"You believe they are the same?" Prometheus asked, watching him closely.

"There must be. They look very similar, but twisted—almost as if they had been dead for days and then risen again.

"I did hear a rumor of such birds being seen in the north. The locals even gave them a name: Strymonides Ornithes, for their proximity to the Strymon River. They said that, at the end of the Thracian wars, the cries of the dying called them. The birds nested high among the cliffs near Amphipolis—watching, feeding, adapting.

"Over time, their wings darkened like stormclouds, and their beaks curved like scythes. Where the Stymphalides were sharp and swift, the Strymonides grew cruel and cunning. They learned not only to pierce flesh, but to mimic the sounds of battle—cries for mercy, of soldiers, of comrades. But I never believed it. Not until now."

"How can you be certain it is the same flock?" Prometheus inquired.

"They say the birds took flight—northward, over the hills of Mount Oeta and through the wilds of central Thessaly, until they reached the River Strymon. There, they found blood enough to drink. And it makes sense now. These lands were littered with corpses during the wars. If there were one place these accursed birds would call home, it would be here."

Heracles said this and slowly released a heavy breath.

"You could not have known. It is not your fault," Prometheus said.

"I do not know—maybe. But I do know this: you need to remember how to fight properly," he said, raising his head to Prometheus. "Starting tomorrow, we train every chance we get. Agreed?"

Prometheus nodded slowly for a moment before asking, "Does the plan remain the same?"

"No. We were lucky before. As far as I understand, like most birds, they don't see well at night—that's the only reason I believe they withdrew. Neither the forest nor the mountains are safe; both could serve as their lair. This place was perfect for defense, with the mountain at our back. On the other side of the range, there's more forest—just as dense, if not denser, if I'm not mistaken. Better not risk another attack."

"What are we doing then?"

"If we head directly south along the mountain range, we can avoid the forest while keeping the slopes at our back if needed. At the end of the range, there's a village called Stagira. It's encircled by forest, but far less dense than what surrounds us here. We can stop there before taking the main road. It will certainly add several days to our journey, but I do not want to gamble with our luck," Heracles said, wiping his blade clean of the thin layer of blood. "Go ahead and rest. I'll take the first watch."

Prometheus did not comment. He simply held his gaze on the fire for a while, then lay down and did not stir until morning.

Heracles never woke him, nor did he sleep. When Prometheus rose, he found him silently gathering their equipment and provisions. He said nothing—only got up and helped with the rest of their belongings.

The following days of travel were uneventful. Each evening, after they made camp, Heracles sparred with Prometheus using two sticks he had carved from sturdy oak.

Prometheus' stance was heavy, and his movements slow, clumsy, and graceless. Yet his grip was solid, and his footing mostly sound. It was clear he had once known how to fight, though most of that knowledge had faded. Still, Heracles could see the old instincts beginning to resurface—painfully slow, but steady.

Heracles did not push him hard. They were still far from Colchis, and there would be time enough for training along the way. While Heracles was likely not the finest swordmaster, he was undoubtedly a skilled warrior—especially with a blade in hand.

His father, Amphitryon—seeking a master to instruct his son in the art of war—sent word to Tyndareus, king of legendary Sparta and his trusted ally. In answer, Tyndareus entrusted the task to his own son, Castor.

Renowned for his skill in horsemanship and warfare, Castor was especially celebrated for his swordsmanship. Among mortal fighters, he was considered one of the very best—if not the best of them all.

Most fighters of that time rarely used both hands on a sword, as the xiphos—their weapon of choice—was typically short in length. A round shield, meanwhile, was the natural companion, offering all the defense a warrior might need.

Castor rarely used a shield, and his sword was longer than a xiphos. Though he typically fought one-handed, his style—uncommon for that time—used the free hand to deliver overhead strikes with added force.

But there was more to Castor's swordsmanship than skill alone. His mother had been a healer—skilled in binding wounds and in the knife-work passed down through generations of those who labored to keep the dying alive. From childhood, she had taught him everything she knew about the mortal body. As a result, Castor understood every vital section of a man's anatomy, and knew precisely where a slash or thrust would be fatal.

His signature move would begin with his blade held upright. As the enemy struck, he would angle his sword into the incoming blow, redirecting its momentum just enough to throw the attack off course. Without breaking motion, he would continue the arc, circling the blade around himself with the edge angled downward. As the sword entered its descending path in a diagonal slash, he placed his second hand on the grip and pulled, adding extra force to the finishing blow.

Castor pushed Heracles hard, teaching him his own way of the sword. Some might have said he was too rough with the young Heracles, and his methods were unconventional at the very least—but the brutal training paid off in the end.

Heracles absorbed everything Castor had to teach, and even advanced the technique—refining it until he used both hands at all times, making every parry and strike at least twice as powerful.

After nearly a week of travel, they finally reached the main road to Stagira, which cut through the forest. The village was completely hidden amidst the trees, even if Heracles had been right about the vegetation being less wild. The trees were still tall and thick enough to conceal everything from a distance, and this was one of the reasons Stagira had never been conquered or sacked during the Thracian Wars.

Moving large armies through the forest had been nearly impossible—especially when trying to defend against an ambush, which could be laid almost anywhere along the road.

As evening fell, they stopped a few miles short of the village and made camp a few hundred yards off the road, in a small clearing where a narrow stream wound through the trees.

After they made preparations for the night, Heracles motioned to Prometheus that it was time for their usual training.

Within only a few days, Heracles had noticed a slight improvement in Prometheus' footwork—but not as much in blocking, and even less in deflecting, parrying, or riposting. Still, it was progress.

Heracles came in with a wide, high sweep—perfect for deflecting or ducking beneath. But Prometheus chose to block it directly, creating a clinch. It was a move suited for catching one's breath, measuring the opponent, and thinking through the next strike.

However, clinching demanded more strength than technique, and Heracles took advantage. He slid his stick against Prometheus' grip, locked it, and pushed him back—disarming him in the same motion. As Prometheus stumbled, Heracles caught him by the ankle with his foot and swept him aside like fallen grain beneath a blade.

Heracles sighed. “Come on!” he groaned, drawing out the second o with a note of irritation. “Lean on your strengths, not your weaknesses. That strike was perfect for deflecting. I told you—wide slashes are highly telegraphed and easy to read,” he said, offering a hand.

Prometheus accepted it, and Heracles pulled him to his feet.

“Focus on the feet—most offensive strikes start there. And never forget the shoulders; that’s where the motion of an attack begins, before the arms ever move,” Heracles said, taking a few steps back and resuming his stance.

However, something in his peripheral vision caught his attention—a small figure. As he tried to focus in that direction, Prometheus’ stick struck him hard in the shoulder, snapping Heracles’ head toward him.

“Seriously?” Heracles said, gesturing with his arms.

Prometheus did not respond. He simply shrugged, a slight, playful smirk on his face.

Heracles turned toward the trees lining the nearby road, his eyes narrowing as his stance shifted.

"Someone's coming," Heracles said, stepping in front of him.

The figure became clear as it slowly approached—a young boy, clothes torn and hanging loose from his thin frame. His steps were uneven, and dirt clung to his skin. He looked as though he might fall with the next breath. As Heracles moved to help, the boy collapsed to the ground.

He rushed to him and found the boy unconscious. Leaning close, Heracles pressed his ear to the boy's mouth—his breathing was faint but steady. He checked the boy's body for wounds but found no serious injuries, only scratches and bruises.

"Is he alive?" Prometheus asked, slightly shaken by the sight.

"Yes. He's just exhausted," Heracles replied, lifting the boy into his arms and heading back toward the camp.

"What happened to him, you think?"

"I do not know," Heracles said, his tone sharpening. "But you can bet I'll find out."

After tending to the boy's wounds, Heracles laid him beside the fire and covered him with his fur. The boy's ragged breathing persisted through the night—until, just before dawn, he abruptly woke screaming.

The cries jolted Prometheus from his sleep. Heracles was already kneeling beside the boy, hands raised in caution.

"Easy there—we mean you no harm. Take a breath. Everything is alright. You're safe now," Heracles said to the boy as gently as he could, while the child scrambled across the ground, kicking and flailing as he tried to crawl backward in panic.

"Take it easy. No one can hurt you now," Heracles added, keeping his hands raised and remaining still, giving the boy space to feel safe in his terrified state.

"Tell us—what happened to you?" Heracles asked. "Maybe we can help."

The boy's frightened expression gradually softened as he studied them with wide, wary eyes. Realizing he was in no immediate danger, he slowly got to his feet.

"Are you hungry? I'd wager you are. My name is Heracles—and honestly, I'm always hungry," he added with a small grin. "This is Prometheus. He's my friend."

Heracles took a few oranges from one of the knapsacks and sat down by the fire.

"Come. Pray, sit," Heracles said, offering the boy one of the oranges.

The boy hesitated at first, but eventually approached the fire and sat down beside them. He accepted the orange cautiously, then bit into it without even peeling it first—something so strange it took Heracles by surprise.

"So, what's your name?" Heracles asked.

"Iphitos," the boy mumbled between hungry bites.

Heracles paused. "What did you say your name was?"

"Iphitos," the boy repeated, fruit juice shimmering on his chin—unaware that Heracles' jaw had slackened.

Prometheus glanced sideways at him. "You know the name?"

"A long time ago..." Heracles muttered. "I... knew a man who bore it."

A moment passed. The boy, having zealously devoured his meal, began licking his hands.

"Do you want another one?" Heracles asked.

The boy turned to him, his face now clear of fear. “Could I?” he said, eyes widening, eyebrows lifting—his childish innocence nearly restored.

Heracles handed him another, and this time the boy took his time peeling the orange.

“So, are you ready to tell us what happened?” Heracles asked.

The boy’s face darkened, but he did not stop peeling the orange.

“My sister,” he said at last.

“What about your sister?” Prometheus asked, joining the conversation.

“They killed her,” the boy whispered, then began sniffling.

“Who did?” Heracles asked gently.

“The people in the mountain. They took her. Nobody ever comes back from there.”

Heracles leaned toward him. “Who are these people? Which mountain? Where are your parents?”

The boy wiped his nose on his sleeve. “They live in the mountain—the one close to the sea, a bit far from the village. Daddy goes there sometimes to pray.”

“Do you mean the temple of Poseidon on Mount Athos?”

“Yes! Daddy says Poseidon protects us, but Mama says it’s Artemis. She says the sea’s never done much for us—only the forest has.”

“How old are you? And your sister?”

“I’m seven. My sister’s bigger. Nine—I think.”

“Why are you so far from the village?”

“Because Daddy wanted to take me to that place, like he did with my sister. But all the kids who go there… they never come back. So I ran,” the boy said, finally peeling off the last of the orange’s skin.

“I see. Alright—stay here. I need to talk to my friend. And here—have another one,” Heracles said, handing him a third orange.

The boy looked up and smiled at him, tears and snot running down his face, mixing with the sticky juice smeared across his cheeks.

Heracles watched the boy chew slowly, the sweetness clinging to his small hands—like innocence itself. His gaze turned hard.

“You know what’s happening here, right?” Heracles said to Prometheus, a few yards away from Iphitos.

"I think I do. How far is the mountain?" Prometheus asked.

"A few days, in the wrong direction. Maybe more. But it does not matter—we're going. Not before we stop at the village."

"What are you going to do?"

Heracles did not answer right away. He simply turned, the firelight catching in his eyes.

"They'll understand soon enough," he said, and walked back toward the boy.

Behind him, Prometheus sighed deeply and looked to the sky.

A storm was gathering above the village—but the one rising below would reach it first.

CHAPTER FIFTEEN

A FEAST FOR THE GODS

Black clouds veiled the sky, blotting out the moonlight and concealing the stars above. A flash of lightning split the horizon in the distance, followed by a low rumble of thunder as they entered the village of Stagira.

Iphitos stayed close to Heracles, never leaving his side. The village seemed deserted, and the eerie silence in the deepening dark made the boy draw even nearer to him.

As they approached the village square, they saw a gathering of torches—each flame flickering weakly against the heavy gloom settling with the storm.

"We need to find my boy," a woman pleaded to an aged man. "It's night, and there are wolves about—we've got to go look for him, pray."

"We will. Worry not," the old man replied, his voice calm and measured. "I have gathered all who can hold a torch or blade."

There was something in the way he spoke—an authority that set him apart from the others.

As they drew nearer, Heracles and Prometheus paused. Iphitos took a step toward the crowd—but froze after only a few paces, halting in front of them.

"Iphitos!" the woman cried out, starting to rush toward him.

The boy hesitated, then slowly backed away and slipped behind Heracles, hiding in the shadow of the towering figure.

"Iphitos," the woman said, stopping a few yards from the trio. "It is me—your mother."

"Boy!" barked a man stepping up behind her. "Get away from those men and listen to your mother."

But the boy did not move an inch. Heracles gently nudged him forward, but Iphitos clung to his tunic with small, trembling hands, refusing to let go.

"Are you his parents?" Heracles asked calmly, as lightning flared in the distance.

The man's eyes flicked between his son and the two strangers beside him, while thunder rolled in from afar.

"What is it to you?" he muttered—more irritated than relieved that his son was safe.

"Did you try to send your son to the temple?" Heracles asked, his voice still calm.

"We beg your mercy, my lord," the mother said, dropping to her knees. "We had no choice."

"Why are you meddling in our lives?" the man snapped, casting a look of scorn at his wife.

"This is not the first time, is it?" Heracles went on. "You sent your daughter first."

"Yes... yes, we did. May the gods forgive us. We—we did not know what else to do. You brought him back—we are grateful, truly. Just... pray, let him go," the woman said through sobs.

"Why're you speakin' to them like that?" the man snapped. "You do not owe them nothin'."

All the while, the village elder and the gathered mob remained silent, watching as they slowly approached—holding their breath with every step.

"You should," Heracles said, fixing his gaze on the man.

A chill crept down the man's spine as he met Heracles' eyes, which now betrayed the edge of his patience.

The man swallowed hard. "They told us that if we did not offer our children, the wrath of Poseidon would destroy the village," he muttered, lowering his head.

"Did Poseidon himself tell you that?" Heracles asked. "What exactly changed for the better after you sacrificed your daughter? Did your nets come back full? Did the storms part? Or are you simply too frightened to question those who claim to speak for the gods?"

As he finished, a crack of thunder tore through the sky—louder than any before.

"But the gods protect us. It is the way it has always been. Who are we to defy them?" the man said, humility and regret finally surfacing in his voice.

"If your gods demand the sacrifice of innocent children," Heracles said, "then your gods are evil."

A flash of lightning lit the sky—followed a breath later by a thunderclap that shook the ground.

"Pray, my lord—have mercy. We swear to repent. We will never do it again. Pray, return my son to me," the woman said, looking up at Heracles, her eyes red from weeping.

"This is not divinity," Prometheus said, as the first drops of rain finally reached the village. "This is fear dressed as faith."

"Go to them," Heracles said to Iphitos, offering a reassuring smile and a nod.

The boy released his grip on Heracles and slowly made his way toward his mother, glancing back and forth between her and Heracles.

He reached her, and she opened her arms, pulling him into a tight embrace, still sobbing.

“Praise the gods for bringing him back to me,” the woman whispered.

“The gods had nothing to do with it,” Heracles said, already turning away. “The gods do not care about you. And I will prove it.”

But before they could leave, the—until now silent—mob moved to block their path. Armed with sickles, pitchforks, and hammers, they stood clustered behind the village elder.

“You shamed us. You offended our gods. You will not walk away without answering for it,” the elder said, his voice burning with fury.

Behind him, the mob stood firm, their torches casting a flickering glow across faces twisted with wrath.

The rain began to fall harder, hissing as it struck the torches, their flames whipping beneath the downpour.

Heracles swept his gaze across them. There were at least twenty—armed, tense, and ready to die for nothing but fear.

"Take a good look, old man. Not so wise, are you?" Heracles growled, his temper barely held in check. "Do I look like someone you want to cross?"

He stepped forward.

"I'll make it simple. Let us pass—and if I hear one whisper, one breath, that another child has been sent to that mountain, I will return. I will burn your village to the ground. And I will bury your gods beneath its ash."

The elder opened his mouth to speak—but whatever words had formed, he swallowed them instead. No one stepped forward.

One by one, the mob began to back away, clearing a path.

Heracles cast a final, menacing look across them. A few lowered their weapons. One man's grip faltered so badly, he soiled himself—just as thunder crashed overhead.

As Heracles and Prometheus turned to leave, Iphitos ran after them, his face streaked with rain and tears.

"Can I come with you?" Iphitos asked, his voice filled with the kind of innocence only a child could carry. "I do not want to stay here."

Heracles knelt before him and smiled gently. "I know. But this road's not meant for children. You've faced too much already. It's time to rest."

"But they'll hurt someone else."

"Not if they believe I'll return. And you needn't worry about those people at the temple—they won't hurt anyone else. Not ever again. I promise you that," Heracles said, gently patting the boy on the head.

"You are brave, Iphitos. Braver than anyone here. Let that be enough—for now," Prometheus added.

"Take my last one," Heracles said, handing the orange to the boy.

Iphitos, the orange clutched in his hands, watched them fade into the darkness—standing alone beneath the heavy rain that now soaked everything around him.

After several miserable days of trudging through mud and treacherous, rain-slicked rocks, they finally reached Mount Athos.

They had exchanged barely a word in all that time. The only things they shared were their muffled breaths beneath the rain and the meager shelter they found along the way.

The rain had not stopped for a single moment—until they reached the temple, where the faint warmth of the sun pierced through the slowly clearing sky.

As the rain faded, the wind died with it, and a stillness settled over the land. The path ahead looked too well-traveled—an observation Heracles forced from his mind.

The temple stood on a cliffside along the mountain, offering a breathtaking view of the Aegean Sea. Though aged, it was well maintained—the white marble that formed its structure bore only faint traces of natural decay.

Standing at the threshold, Heracles paused and turned to Prometheus.

“Take this,” he said, handing Prometheus his knife. “Hopefully you won’t need it—but just in case you must protect yourself.”

Prometheus accepted the knife and tucked it inside his cloak.

They crossed the temple grounds and moved quietly into its depths. Though it seemed deserted—forgotten by time—they pressed on.

At the far end of the structure, they came upon a circular chamber.

Within the chamber stood a towering statue of Poseidon, carved in a triumphant stance, his trident resting upright at his side.

Beneath him lay a marble altar—broad enough to hold a small animal… or a child. Faint smears of dried blood marked its pale surface.

Kneeling around the altar were several acolytes, their heads bowed low in silence. At the center of them all—positioned between the altar and the statue—stood a hooded figure.

He wore a faded red robe that brushed the ground—the kind once worn by priests. One arm was raised high, as though awaiting Poseidon's reply.

"Welcome, children of the gods, to our humble temple," the hooded figure intoned, turning to face them.

He drew back his hood, revealing an old, weathered face—gentle in its lines, with a serene stillness behind the eyes.

"Pray, come. Join us in worship. Poseidon has shown his favor today, lifting the storm and blessing us with smooth seas," he said, extending a graceful hand.

They did not move. Heracles and Prometheus remained still at the center of the chamber.

"Are you the high priest of this temple?" Heracles asked—though he already knew the answer.

"Yes, child, I am," the hierophant replied. "Have you come to revel in our god's glory? All children of the gods are welcome here."

His voice was calm, his expression one of tranquil devotion.

"No. We're here for a different reason," Heracles said.

The hierophant tilted his head slightly. "And what reason would that be, child?"

Heracles took a step forward. "To stop you."

A pause.

"Stop what, child?" the hierophant asked, still unshaken.

Heracles' eyes narrowed. "Do you deny sacrificing children?"

"My child, we do no such thing," the hierophant said gently. "We offer only our hearts to the gods—and sometimes, they grant us gifts for our faith. Nothing more."

"I can see the dried blood on the altar from here," Heracles said, his patience wearing dangerously thin.

"Is it sacrifice," the hierophant asked humbly, "to free a soul from its earthly bonds and send it to the divine bosom of the eternal gods? We are but instruments of their will—faithful servants who live only to celebrate their glory."

"This isn't faith," Heracles said, jaw tightening. "It's blind obedience to madness. The gods couldn't care less."

"They have not," Prometheus added quietly, "not for a long time now."

"I've heard enough," Heracles said, his tone edged with finality. "Let me put it simply—either you stop slaughtering innocent children, or I'll burn this temple to the ground."

"My child," the hierophant replied, spreading his arms. "Join us. Revel in the embrace of the gods. Only they can fill your heart with joy. United, we shall bring peace and prosperity to these lands."

The hierophant smiled. "One to save many."

Heracles stepped closer.

"Yes, my child—come. Be one with us," he said, nodding gently as Heracles advanced.

Prometheus remained where he was, his eyes on the kneeling acolytes, their heads still bowed low.

When only a few steps remained between them, Heracles stopped.

He drew his sword and raised it, the blade pointing directly at the hierophant.

He said nothing. He did not need to.

“Will you strike down faithful instruments of the gods’ will?” the hierophant asked, his voice calm, his eyes unflinching. “Will you raise your sword against faith itself—against the gods?”

“I will,” Heracles said. “I am.” He leveled the blade. “Flee. Now.”

“Flee?” the hierophant echoed, his tone shifting—softness curdling into something strange. “Why would I flee? I like it here. The scent of blood mingled with sea air is... well, invigorating.”

Heracles frowned, his sword still fixed on the hierophant.

“Oh, come now, don’t be shy,” the hierophant said, his voice curling at the edges. “Who doesn’t enjoy a bit of children’s flesh now and then? The fear they carry just before death—mmm—it seeps into the meat like seasoning.”

He closed his eyes and smiled. “My, oh my... I’m salivating just thinking about it.”

Then his expression twitched, and something in his face shifted—subtle at first, but wrong.

“But enough daydreaming. Adult flesh will do just fine for today. What say you, children?” He tilted his head toward the kneeling figures. “Feeling hungry?”

And with a blink—

—the illusion shattered.

It broke like glass—a hundred mirror fragments crashing down in silence, revealing the truth beneath.

The marble faded. The chamber blackened.

What once gleamed white was now slick with rot. Filth caked every surface; bones were stacked in the corners like discarded kindling.

The scent of salt was gone. Now, it was blood and bile.

In an instant, the acolytes rose from their knees. They looked like children now—silent, smiling, their eyes glowing faintly in the dark.

And the hierophant was a priest no longer.

What stood before them now was a creature twisted into the shape of a woman—part serpent, part corpse.

Her face was etched with deep, unnatural lines that writhed when she moved. Her hair hung in thick, matted cords, as though stitched together from strands that never grew—only knotted and fused over time.

Her eyes were reptilian in shape, but colorless. Just two pits of glistening black—empty and unblinking.

"What in Tartarus are you?" Heracles asked, his nose wrinkling at the stench—like rotting blood and spoiled meat baked in the sun.

"Ah, yes. Silly me," she said, tilting her head, her smile stretching far too wide. "I forgot to introduce myself."

She spread her arms in mock welcome. "I'm Mormo. Welcome to my humble—if rather cozy—little abode."

Her tone dropped—sing-song and sharp. "Now, before we feast on your very sweet, very tender flesh—though not quite as sweet as the children who came before—may I ask something?"

She looked to Prometheus, then back to Heracles. "You, old man... you probably won't taste good at all. But worry not—we'll eat you anyway."

She dragged her tongue slowly across the length of one blackened fingernail, the claw glistening with something dark and wet.

"Are you—?"

But before she could finish, Heracles lunged. In a blur, his sword drove deep into her scaled belly, the blade sinking to the guard.

"Enough," he growled, standing mere inches from her twisted form.

His eyes burned with fury, his face carved in disgust.

"Taste metal, abomination."

"Mmm... Olympian metal," Mormo purred, glancing down at the blade still lodged in her flesh. "Bitter. Not to my liking. But as you wish, my... child."

With a sudden motion, she shoved Heracles in the chest, sending him flying across the chamber.

"Feed, my children," she hissed.

The once-frozen, smiling children lifted their heads in unison.

Then, without a sound, they opened their mouths—wide—skin splitting from the corners of their lips up to their ears, revealing rows of razor-sharp teeth that had no place in any mortal jaw.

"Prometheus!" Heracles shouted as he rose from the ground. "Watch my back!"

Without waiting, he charged straight toward Mormo.

One of the child-like creatures leapt at him mid-sprint, but with a single, fluid motion, Heracles swung his sword—severing its head clean off.

Both body and head hit the ground with a dull thud.

Mormo hissed, her mouth stretching wide as she revealed her long, snake-like tongue—thin, black, and forked at the tip.

Prometheus rushed to follow, but the creatures swarmed forward, blocking his path.

Heracles closed the distance and slashed at Mormo with measured force—but her serpent-like reflexes made her faster than he expected.

She twisted aside, her body bending with unnatural grace, and struck back with a flurry of blows from her clawed, blackened fingers—each one sharp as a dagger.

Heracles deflected most of them with his sword, steel clashing against nail with a harsh, metallic scrape.

But her rapid, snaking movements kept him off balance; a few strikes slipped through. One tore through his sleeve. Another carved a shallow line across his ribs. His tunic hung in tatters, streaked with thin trails of red.

Prometheus was forced back by the slow, unnerving advance of the child-like creatures. Saliva dripped from their wide, gaping jaws as they moved in eerie silence, their steps perfectly in sync. They formed a line across the chamber, splitting it in two—dividing the battleground between him and Heracles.

Heracles grunted in frustration as he parried another swipe from Mormo's claws, then countered with a brutal slash that severed her hand at the wrist.

She shrieked and staggered back, clutching the bleeding stump as black ichor spurted across the stone floor. But she did not retreat—instead, her body coiled low like a serpent ready to strike.

Heracles lunged for the killing blow.

Mormo ducked under his blade and surged forward with her jaws wide open, fangs bared and snapping.

Before her teeth could sink into his throat, Heracles caught her by the neck with one hand

and slammed her to the ground, pinning her beneath him.

With a roar, he raised his sword and began hammering it down against her face—once, twice, a third time—each blow cracking bone and splitting flesh.

Then, hissing, she lashed out—her tongue darting from her broken mouth to slither across his cheek, cold and slick as a snake dragged over stone.

"Mmm... delicious. More. More," Mormo whispered, as though savoring the violence itself.

Heracles did not stop. He kept pummeling his sword down until her face was nothing but ruin—her once-repulsive features beaten into a shapeless smear.

Across the chamber, Prometheus fought to keep the child-like creatures at bay, kicking and shoving them aside. But eventually, his back hit the wall.

With nowhere left to retreat, he drew the knife Heracles had given him.

As one of the creatures crept closer, jaws trembling in anticipation, Prometheus drove the blade straight into its forehead—burying it to the hilt.

The creature stiffened. Then its limbs went slack, and it collapsed to the floor in a lifeless heap.

Mormo, her face now misshapen and half-caved in beneath Heracles' blows, lay dazed and gasping.

Still, she tried to reach him—her long, black, forked tongue slithering toward his cheek like a dying thing.

But Heracles caught it in his hand. With a sharp twist and a violent pull, he ripped it clean from her bloody mouth and flung it to the floor.

She screamed.

He raised his sword, muscles coiled to bring it down and finish her once and for all—

And then, she spoke.

"No... let me go," she gurgled through her shattered mouth, each word choked in blood.

"Spare me, and I'll grant you the offerings... the treasures..."

Heracles stared down at her, unmoved.

"Sure. I'll let you… back to the abyss that spat you out. Now die."

He drove his sword between her eyes, the blade punching through bone and deep into the marble beneath.

The remaining child-like creatures lunged at Prometheus—

—but stopped mid-step.

They lifted their heads in eerie unison, mouths stretching open wide.

Then came the sound: a single, piercing hiss that rose into a scream—high, shrill, and unnatural. It echoed off the stone walls, so sharp and grating that both Heracles and Prometheus clutched their ears in pain.

And then, silence.

The creatures collapsed where they stood, falling lifeless to the cold stone floor.

They looked at each other—bloodied, bruised, but still standing.

Once more, they had survived a nightmare.

Heracles exhaled slowly. “Let’s get out of here.”

Outside, they stepped into the fading light.

Heracles walked to the edge of the cliff and gazed out over the sea—calm, silver, serene.

In that moment, he hated it.

CHAPTER SIXTEEN
REALIZATION IN BLOOD

After a couple of weeks of traveling along the lonely coast from Mount Athos, Heracles and Prometheus reached the weather-beaten cliffs and oak-covered forests between Amphipolis and Krenides, where sea mist clung to the air and the cries of distant gulls faded into the splash of the waves.

The journey was longer along the sandy beaches, but Heracles thought it wiser to avoid the main road and any further unwanted encounters. The coastal path offered flatter ground and a clear view of the inland hills—making it easier to spot anyone who might be trailing them.

Heracles was fully healed by now, save for the wounds he had recently received from Mormo. He had already removed the bandages, letting the cuts breathe, and the daily swims in the salty sea had done wonders for them.

Neither of the two spoke of the encounter with Mormo, nor did they discuss its aftermath. Both had been marked by the ordeal, and the memory of slaying monsters that wore the faces of children was something they each struggled to forget.

As the sun began its descent, chilly, rough winds stirred from the northwest, turning the sea's surface into a shifting canvas of dark blue and white as waves rose and broke against the shore.

They decided to move away from the beach and seek shelter in the forest to the north. There, the wind would be less of a nuisance, and they could more easily make camp for the night.

The past few weeks had been enough for Heracles to forget how much he loathed traversing dense forests—but thankfully, this particular one was sparse in vegetation and almost perfect for hunting.

"I think I'll go hunting today," Heracles said aloud.

"Do you wish me to come?" Prometheus asked.

"Eh, no. You don't have to."

"As you will. Are we making camp for the night?"

"Soon. I'm looking for a good spot."

After a while, Heracles found the perfect place for the night—beneath a large oak, its canopy dense enough to shield them from the weather.

They made their usual preparations and sat down by the fire. Heracles readied his bow and arrows, then pulled out a whetstone to sharpen his sword. With slow, methodical strokes, he began honing the blade's edge, focusing especially on the point—the very one he had recently driven into marble.

"I meant to ask you—does it bear a name? Your sword?" Prometheus watched him guide the whetstone with care.

"It does," Heracles said, his focus unbroken.

"I can read the engravings. They carry power—but no name I recognize."

"The name was given when it was forged."

"Well? Care to share it?"

"It is called…" He paused, then said, "Teraxion."

"Te-ra-xion. I see—an instrument meant to end monsters, or a blade forged to slay beasts. A fitting name," Prometheus said, tossing a piece of wood into the fire. "I did not know you spoke the divine tongue."

"I don't. I can understand some, but that's all," Heracles said, continuing to sharpen. "My friend Medea—the one you'll soon meet—speaks it well. Almost perfectly."

“Very well. How long do you think until we reach Colchis?”

“I’m not sure. A month? Maybe more?” Heracles said, continuing with zeal.

Just a few miles behind them, at the edge of the forest, Pandora stopped and gazed into the distance. It had been some time since they disappeared among the trees—the first time she had lost sight of them since they departed the temple at Mount Athos.

She hesitated, uncertain how to proceed. With the light fading, searching for them inside the forest could prove difficult—or even dangerous, if they sensed they were being followed.

All this time, she had kept her distance—far enough not to betray her divinity—watching for the perfect opportunity to strike, even as she continued to wrestle with the nature of her quest. Now, though, seemed a good time to mask herself, to avoid any premature encounter with them.

She closed her eyes and concentrated. This was her first time attempting such a spell. She had never needed to hide her identity before, and attempting unfamiliar magic was never easy—

sometimes even dangerous. Still, she saw no other option.

It took her some time, but in the end she managed to alter her appearance—just enough. Her eyes now mirrored those of a mortal, and the glow of her divinity lay hidden behind the veil of the spell.

"This should be enough," she thought, taking a steady breath, then stepped quietly into the forest.

The spell introduced several approaches she had not considered before. A risky frontal assault might now be avoided. Perhaps these woods offered a unique opportunity—to lay an ambush, or even pose as a lost woman in distress—to lure them in.

The thought alone curdled in her chest and left a bitter taste in her mouth. She did not want to do this—not truly. But she knew she must. The Titans had been responsible for her parents' death, and Prometheus was one of them. Perhaps the last, but still a Titan. Even so, the idea of deception and murder was hard to stomach. She had no choice. It had to be done—for Hera, and for her parents.

As she cautiously moved through the forest, scanning the surroundings for the duo, she heard a twig snap in the distance. She paused and waited, listening carefully to make sure it was nothing. No other sound followed—only the wind whispering through the foliage high above.

She resumed her search when, all of a sudden, a dark figure burst out from behind her and lunged forward.

Caught by surprise, Pandora did not turn fast enough to avoid the incoming blow. The figure crashed into her, sending her tumbling across the forest floor.

"Φῶς," she whispered, and light flared around her in an instant.

A guttural howl ripped through the undergrowth as she lifted her gaze—just in time to see a misshapen figure lurch backward into the trees. It stood on two legs, but barely—its frame twisted, draped in patchy, matted fur. The creature's limbs were too long, its shoulders hunched, its face caught between man and wolf—an elongated snout and yellowing fangs. Its eyes shrank from the light as it threw up a clawed arm to shield them.

She rose quickly while the beast was still reeling from the light, and with a violent thrust of her hand, unleashed a force strong enough to send it hurtling through the air. It crashed into a tree with a bone-jarring thud, followed by a faint, broken howl that shook the trunk and sent a shower of acorns tumbling to the ground.

A piercing pain shot through her, and a bitter liquid rose in her throat. She touched her lips and saw them stained with blood. Reaching with her other hand toward the sharp throb in her back, she realized what she had failed to notice before—the beast had clawed her, deep. She could feel four long, parallel slashes torn through her tunic, blood warm as it streamed down her spine.

The beast shook off the blow, rose to its hind legs, and let out a howl so savage it made her hair stand on end.

She wiped the blood from her mouth and braced for the charge. The creature lunged forward, crawling on all fours—only to be stopped by a single, searing word.

"Πῦρ," she uttered, and from her fingertips, flames poured forth, flooding the woods in white and crimson light.

The fire stopped the beast in its tracks as its right arm caught ablaze, burning away the long, coarse hair in an instant and releasing a foul stench of scorched flesh and singed fur.

It recoiled several yards in a panic, thrashing its flaming arm against the dirt. As it struggled to smother the fire, the flames at Pandora's fingertips began to dim, their intensity fading with each breath.

A strange weightlessness crept into her skull, as if her thoughts were slipping loose. Fog thickened in her vision, shapes at the edges smearing into shadow. Her knees buckled. The forest tilted. She caught herself—barely.

The beast had managed to extinguish the flames and now hunched over, licking its scorched arm in quick, jerking motions. It lifted its head and locked eyes with Pandora, baring sharp teeth as its lips drew back and its massive jaw tensed—a low growl rising from deep within its throat.

Slowly, the creature rose to its full height with a heavy, purposeful motion and let out a sharp snort. At that same moment, Pandora's legs gave out beneath her, and she dropped to her knees.

Straining to keep her eyes open, she could only watch as the beast advanced, each step laden with menace. Her body failed her entirely, and she pitched forward, the forest floor rushing up to meet her.

She had never imagined this would be the end. The mortal world was not like the one above the clouds. There was no peace here—only pain, blood, and the weight of flesh.

A sharp whistle cut through the air as an arrow flew past Pandora and struck the beast high in the chest. It let out a pained howl and clawed at the shaft, but before it could wrench it free, Heracles stepped from the shadows and loosed a second arrow that buried itself deep in the creature's thigh.

Without breaking stride, he flung the bow aside, drew his sword from his hip and shield from his back, and charged.

Wounded and reeling, the beast lunged to strike—only to be stopped by the crash of Heracles' shield. With a powerful shove, he knocked it off balance and followed with a swift thrust, driving the blade straight into its upper body. The metal pierced clean through its muscular abdomen—but even that did not stop it.

The beast attacked frantically, striking with both arms in unison, but Heracles blocked each blow with ease. He held firm behind his shield, deflecting strike after strike until the creature's strength began to wane—its wounds and fatigue slowing it down.

Seizing the moment, Heracles slammed the edge of his shield into the beast's face, dazing it.

Without pause, he followed through with a swift, angled slash across the neck—Castor's signature move. The blade carved through flesh and split the main artery in its throat.

Blood poured from the wound, soaking its long black fur as it stumbled back.

"Is there a shred of mortality left in you?" Heracles asked, his voice low.

The beast looked at him with dark, wolven eyes—and growled, deep and hollow. There was nothing in its gaze but raw, animal fury, as if every trace of reason had long since been devoured by the curse.

"Forgive me, son of Lykaon," Heracles said, sorrow threading through his voice. "But this has to end."

With a swift step, he closed the distance and drove his sword deep into the beast's chest, piercing its heart. The creature released a long, mournful howl to the sky—but before the sound had faded, Heracles wrenched the blade free and, in one fluid motion, swept it wide across its neck, severing the beast's head and cutting the howl short.

Pandora watched through blurred vision, drifting at the edge of consciousness when she sensed someone near. It was Prometheus, kneeling beside her, checking on her with quiet urgency.

Heracles approached, his voice rough with exertion. "Is she all right?"

"You... saved me..." she managed to whisper, before darkness took her and the world slipped away.

CHAPTER SEVENTEEN
THE THREAD DRAWS TIGHT

The deep night embraced the flickering fire at their camp, where Heracles and Prometheus passed their quiet hours. The wind had stilled, and the woods lay hushed once more, wrapped in their familiar peace.

Heracles had placed Pandora close to the fire and carefully tended her wounds, washing them and applying a mixture of crushed herbs and pale flowers the Muses had given for such times.

The substance resembled the one Medea had used on him back in Colchis, after his fight with the Sirens, but its fragrance was vastly different. Where Medea's had smelled of roses—deliberate, refined—this one carried the scent of a wild valley in bloom, untamed and alive.

He finished by wrapping her wounds with a clean strip of cloth, then placed a damp one across her forehead. She was burning with fever, and her breathing had grown so faint it barely stirred the air.

"Will she live?" Prometheus asked, his eyes on Pandora as she slept.

"I don't know. I hope she does," Heracles replied, then bit into the last apple—soft, bruised, and barely edible.

"How did you know? You ran the moment you heard the howl."

"I hunted a son of Lykaon before. Most of them are dead, and this one may well have been the last," Heracles said, the corner of his lip tightening with sorrow.

"Lykaon? Who was he?" Prometheus asked, brow furrowed.

"It's not a pleasant story. Do you truly wish to hear it?"

"More unpleasant than the temple?"

"Mormo was a fairytale—something parents whispered to frighten their children into obedience. I never knew such a creature truly existed. But she did. A nightmare in flesh. The myth was true: she consumed children, and with their souls, she crafted her own twisted offspring. I do not want to speak of it."

"Then speak of Lykaon instead."

"Sometimes I forget how little you know of monsters. Must be nice."

"Perhaps," Prometheus said with a heavy sigh. "Though I know the Daimons—and believe me, the memory of the monsters you speak of, their offspring and all, is far easier to bear than the memory of theirs."

"Fine. I'll tell you what I know," Heracles said, taking a deep breath through his nose.

"They say Lykaon ruled Arcadia through strength and fear, siring sons across every valley and hill. No queen, no wife—only power taken, never granted. But it was in war that his fate began to turn.

"He conquered a village from a rival kingdom—small, unarmed, sacred. The people did not fight. They begged. He took what he pleased. Among them was a healer... said to be the last of her line, keeper of forgotten rites. She cursed him with her dying breath. No ritual. No spell. Just words, soaked in blood.

"At first, nothing. But then came the hunger. His sons began to waste away, even as they fed. They devoured flocks. Then herds. Then men. Still their bellies groaned.

"Lykaon grew afraid. Or ashamed. Perhaps both. So he led them into the mountains to pray. He brought them to a stone altar older than any temple, hoping to beg for forgiveness... or find a cure."

Heracles paused. The fire cracked.

"But the hunger followed.

"They turned on him—tore into him with their bare hands and teeth. And when they came back down, they were changed. Limbs too long. Fur in patches. Voices more howl than word.

"Lykaon died on that mountain. Or worse—he lived, remembering every bite.

"They say you can still hear them on cold nights. Not howling at the moon—but at their own empty bellies."

Prometheus did not interrupt once. He simply listened, the fire crackling beside him, mingling with the ragged sound of Pandora's breathing.

Late the next morning, Pandora slowly opened her eyes. The fog had lifted from her vision, and color was beginning to return. She struggled to rise, just as Heracles came into view.

"What are you doing? You need to rest," he said, crouching beside her.

"Who... are you?" she asked, struggling to hold her composure while hiding the truth behind her eyes.

"My name is Heracles, son of Amphitryon and Alcmene. This is Prometheus, son of—"

"It does not matter," Prometheus said, stepping into her view.

"What happened?" she asked.

"Well, a son of Lykaon attacked you. But you need not worry about him anymore. What were you doing alone in the woods at night?" Heracles asked.

"I thought the woods would offer..." She paused, wincing as pain flashed across her face when she tried to sit up. "Some shelter from the weather. Just enough to last the night."

"I see. But why were you alone?" Heracles pressed.

"I can handle myself," she said.

"We know that. You're a sorceress. Still, that beast had been crawling through the woods for who knows how long. You were fortunate."

"Fortunate? Wait—how do you know I'm a sorceress?"

"You mean besides the freshly burned arm of the beast? There was a huge ball of light above you—until you passed out, that is."

"Of course. I suppose I'm still a bit disoriented," she said, meeting Heracles' gaze first, then

Prometheus'. "I owe you both a debt of gratitude. You saved my life."

"Pff, you owe us nothing. We were just glad we heard the howling in time," Heracles said with a nod and a faint smile. "Where are you headed?"

"East. I'm a traveler. I teach magic to gifted girls," she said, uncertain whether the lie would hold.

But it was true—the part about the girls. The gods gave men physical strength. Magic belonged to women. Blood-born, moon-touched, passed down in whispers. And both gods and men feared what women could speak into the world.

"I see. What is your name?"

"Pandora."

"I travel a lot myself. Never heard of you."

"Do you know all the sorceresses in the Known World?" she asked, raising an eyebrow.

Heracles exhaled a short laugh through his nose. "You're right—I don't. But I can recognize the attitude of one. And you definitely have it."

"Forgive me—my back is killing me."

"No need. Truth is, you remind me of someone I know—mostly the fire in you," he said with a slight grin. "Perhaps you've heard of her. Her name is Medea."

"Of course. Not in person, but by legend—her and Kirke. I always hoped to meet them."

Heracles paused for a moment. Under any other circumstance, he would never share his path with a stranger. But sorceresses had a way of earning his trust—not through charm, but presence. And there was something about Pandora that echoed Medea—not in looks, but in bearing, in the quiet weight she carried.

It was not blind trust. It was instinct, honed by hardship. She was alone, wounded, and powerful—too dangerous to ignore, and perhaps too useful to leave behind. If she meant harm, he would see it soon enough. Until then, he would keep her close.

"Well, you're in luck. We're headed that way. Would you care to join us? We could use a magic-wielder—and as you've experienced yourself, traveling alone is not always wise. Even for someone like you."

"No. I wouldn't want to burden you further—you've already done more than I could ever repay," she said with quiet sincerity.

And it was true. She was caught between the weight of her duty and the debt she now owed him.

"Then consider this the perfect way to start," Heracles said. "Join us. We keep each other safe. Call it repayment if it makes it easier. And let's be honest—you're in no shape to travel alone. Everyone needs someone to lean on, sometimes."

Pandora did not reply. She nodded, and a faint smile rose to her lips—unbidden, born of warmth she wished she did not feel.

CHAPTER EIGHTEEN
LAUGHTER BENEATH THE BOUGHS

After a couple of days of slow walking, Krenides was still nowhere in sight. Pandora was recovering—her deep wounds had begun to heal quickly—but she remained sluggish, dragging her feet with each step. Heracles stayed close, steadying her whenever she leaned on him for support.

She spoke little—just a few words now and then—and neither Heracles nor Prometheus pressed her. It was clear she was still shaken by the ordeal and her encounter with the beast, so they left her in peace.

Their decision to follow the main road was not made lightly. Heracles' opinion of such routes had not changed—he still avoided them whenever possible—but given Pandora's condition, he had made an exception. The flat, well-worn path would make her steps easier.

Their supplies were running low, and with his last attempt at hunting cut short—and now a third mouth to feed—a stop at a village or town was becoming necessary, though Heracles dreaded the idea.

The only options were hunting or fishing—but he was hopeless with a rod—leaving only the former as a viable choice. Unfortunately, the nearest patch of forest was still a fair distance ahead, and there were no signs of wildlife nearby that might make a proper meal. He could try shooting seagulls if they ventured down toward the beach, but he knew from experience they tasted foul, so he kept that as a last resort.

They stopped to rest for the night in an open field beside the road. Heracles handed over the last piece of fruit—nearly rotten now—to Pandora and Prometheus. They all ate without thinking much of it, and with their stomachs barely satisfied, they slept beneath the moonlit sky.

Heracles' belly groaned so loudly it woke them several times during the night.

"Time to rise," Heracles said softly, though there was a hint of urgency in his tone.

With the sun barely up, both Prometheus and Pandora rose slowly, their expressions betraying a restless night.

"Why are you up this early?" Prometheus asked, rubbing the sleep from his face.

"There's a small forest in the distance. I need the daylight to hunt something down for a meal. I'm starving," he said, rubbing his belly.

"We know. Your stomach kept complaining all through the night," Pandora said mid-yawn.

"Apologies, but if we don't find something soon, I'll shoot every seagull in the area just to find one that doesn't taste like grease-soaked leather left out in the sun—and believe me, you do not want to taste seagull," he added, his face twisting in disgust at the memory.

They made their way toward the forest, which lay only a few miles north, just off the main road. Heracles quickened his pace, nearly carrying Pandora—her feet barely brushing the ground with each stride, as if she floated. Prometheus struggled to keep up.

In less than an hour, they reached the edge of the promised woods, where Heracles paused to ready his equipment.

"Both of you stay here. Hopefully I won't be long. But if, for some reason, I'm late—do not come after me. I'm not leaving this forest without at least a damned rabbit," he said and disappeared into the trees.

He moved silently through the forest, knowing exactly where to place his steps without disturbing anything nearby. Despite his size, he advanced with the ease of a royal huntsman—slipping between roots and shadows as deftly as the finest of them.

A few hours passed with no sign of prey. Though he found the occasional set of tracks, they always led to nothing. Cursing under his breath, he pressed on—surrender was never in his nature.

Eventually, he spotted a series of prints in a patch of bare earth. But these were not animal tracks. They were footprints—several of them—as if a group of men had passed through. He followed them.

The trail led into a deepening silence. Even the birds had gone quiet. The air hung heavy with the scent of torn roots and damp earth.

The tracks led him deeper into the woods. As he pressed on, he began to notice deep holes scattered across the forest floor—irregular and raw. Kneeling to inspect one, he realized they were not natural. These were tree pits—places where trunks had been ripped clean from the earth, roots and all, as if plucked like weeds by something immense.

A storm, perhaps? A passing tornado? That was his first thought. But it made no sense. Why had only certain trees been taken? Why were the others untouched—not even bent, not a single branch broken? Maybe the missing ones had been old, their roots weakened. But that theory quickly crumbled. There was no wind-scarring, no splintered debris, and the surrounding trees stood perfectly undisturbed.

The footprints had vanished beneath churned dirt, fallen leaves, and the tangled remains of torn roots. Still, Heracles followed the trail of destruction.

As he reached the last of the uprooted holes, his instincts were confirmed—this was no natural disaster. The trees had been stripped of their greenery and stacked to form a large, makeshift cage of bare trunks. Inside, huddled close despite the room around them, were several men who looked like miners.

And there it was—broad-shouldered, swaying slightly, humming something low and broken as it toyed with the captives.

Just outside the wooden cell, a towering figure sat on its enormous backside, turned away, holding two miners in each of its massive hands.

"Man hug other man," the creature said, then brought his hands together.

"For the love of Hephaistos, you're crushing us, you dimwit!" one of the miners shouted.

"No talky. Be friends," the creature replied, continuing without the slightest regard for their screams.

Heracles crept forward, slow and deliberate, until he was close enough to see the faces of the struggling miners—twisted in panic as they writhed in its grasp. The others inside the wooden cage were shouting and cursing the creature, their voices rising in desperation.

The monster's fidgeting stopped. A long, wet sniff cut through the shouts and curses echoing between the trees. Then, without warning, its head snapped back, and its single eye—bulbous, bloodshot, and ringed with crusted lashes—locked directly onto Heracles.

"You, man. Why come? Take toys? No, no—my toys. Man go find his own toys," the Kyklōps said, staring at Heracles with its huge, milky-white eye.

"Help us!" one of the miners it was holding shouted.

"You. Shut mouth," the monster growled, then flung the miner back into the cage.

The man landed safely atop the others, groaning. Still gripping the second miner in one hand, the Kyklōps used its now-free hand to rise.

Its body was enormous—filthy skin stretched tight over thick cords of muscle, streaked with mud and flecked with bark. Patches of coarse, matted hair clung to its shoulders and chest, and its limbs moved with an awkward, lumbering rhythm, like a child still learning its strength. As it rose to its full height, its head brushed the low-hanging boughs overhead.

“I tell man—away go,” it said, now looming in full view.

Heracles stepped closer and slung his bow across his back, the string pressed against his chest.

“Greetings,” he said, taking a few more steps forward.

“I like your cage. Did you make it?” he asked, drawing even nearer to the structure.

“Man like cage? Man want get in cage?” the Kyklōps asked, its eye narrowing in confusion.

“No, I’m just admiring your craftsmanship.”

“Why in Tartarus are you talking to him? Can’t you see he’s got water in the brain?” shouted one of the miners from inside the cage.

"Shh, keep it down," Heracles whispered.

"No touchy trees," the Kyklōps said, and Heracles halted—now only a few yards from the cage.

"I'm not touching your trees. What are you going to do with the men?"

"Do?"

"Yes, do! Are you going to eat them?"

"Eat men? Bah. Men no taste good," the Kyklōps said, sticking out its tongue in visible disgust. "Men play. Trakhios show them."

"I see. Well, pardon me, Trakhios—but I need these men," Heracles said.

"No. Men stay. You go," the Kyklōps replied, stamping his foot and shaking the earth.

"Fine. Let's make a deal. You give me these men, and I'll bring you others. Look at them—they're weak, easy to break. I'll bring you many men. Young, strong men. Like me."

"No! Men stay!"

"Do you see this sword?" Heracles said, and the Kyklōps glanced down at his waist. "Either you give me these men, or I'll use it to cut off your hands. Then you won't be able to play with them. Besides, these men talk too much. Young men don't."

The Kyklōps looked as if he were thinking—until, at last, he tossed the man he was holding at Heracles' feet.

"Take man. Bring more men."

"No. I need all of them—to help me bring others. Many men. Willing to play with Trakhios," Heracles said as he helped the miner to his feet.

"Man right. Men talk much. You take men. Bring better men to play," the Kyklōps said, pulling a tree trunk from the cage like it was nothing.

One by one, the miners stepped out and gathered behind Heracles.

"Now go—man be quick. Trakhios make bigger cage."

Heracles started walking away, the miners following close behind.

"Wouldn't it have been easier to just kill him? I mean, look at you—you're almost as big as that Kyklōps," said one of the miners.

"Not even close. And no—he's not a threat. And he let you go, didn't he?" Heracles replied.

"I suppose so. But what if he captures some other poor soul?" asked another.

"Well then, you'd better warn the others—and stay out of these woods," Heracles said.

"But we get wood from this forest. It's the best around for the mine," said another miner.

"Then unless you want to die as playthings for a Kyklōps, I suggest finding another forest."

"Enough, all of you," said the eldest miner. "He just saved our miserable hides, and you're complaining? Give them no mind—we're grateful!"

"Don't mention it. I'm glad you're all unharmed."

"Well, our pride's very harmed," said the miner who had been one of the Kyklōps' playthings not long ago.

"Did I not say to shut it?" said the elder. "How could we ever repay you?"

"Do you have any food?" Heracles asked—just as his stomach growled so loudly that a few of the miners flinched, thinking the Kyklōps had come back for them.

After some time navigating through the woods, they reached the edge, where Prometheus and Pandora waited patiently for his return.

"I thought you went hunting for food, not men," Pandora said, eyeing the crowd gathered behind him.

"They're miners. They work the mountain near Mount Haemus. Their village is northeast of

Stagira, and they've invited us. It's a long story—I'll tell it on the way," Heracles said, picking up his belongings.

The village lay not far, and by nightfall they had arrived. The miners' wives, grateful for the safe return of their husbands, welcomed the group with open arms and prepared a feast fit for a king. Fires were lit, and tables were laid with everything the villagers could offer—fresh bread, wild vegetables, roasted goat, and jugs of dark wine that never seemed to empty.

As the night wore on, one of the miners recounted their rescue with grand embellishments, painting Heracles as a demigod who stared down the Kyklōps with nothing but a glare. The villagers laughed, cheered, and passed around more wine, letting the story grow with each retelling. There was food and drink, song and dance—and for a time, no shadows loomed.

Prometheus and Pandora shared quiet smiles, their burdens briefly forgotten as they joined the revelry. But no one embraced the night quite like Heracles. He did not stop eating or drinking until he could no longer stand—and even then, he kept reaching for leftovers, shoving bread and meat into his mouth with a satisfied groan, his arms limp at his sides, a great grin carved across his face like it belonged there.

CHAPTER NINETEEN

THE PRICE OF FOOLISHNESS

With Krenides behind them, Heracles, Prometheus, and Pandora followed the main coastal road eastward, toward Colchis. The only town that lay between them and their destination was Abdera, perched at the eastern edge of Thrace—a final outpost before the long, desolate stretch leading to the distant kingdom of gold, silver, and jewels.

The miners' wives had kindly packed all the leftovers from their wonderful evening together. It was enough to last them a few weeks, but the road ahead would demand more.

Pandora, who had been lingering behind with Prometheus, quickened her pace and drew up beside Heracles, who was leading the way.

She eyed him carefully.

"So... you are gods, are you not?"

Heracles did not stop walking. "I knew that question was coming."

"Then you should have an answer ready."

He exhaled through his nose. "Why now?"

"I overheard what the miners were whispering—about your peculiar eyes. Yours, and Prometheus'. As far as I know, few have such eyes. I didn't wish to pry when we first met... but tell me. Are you?"

"No."

"Then what are you?"

"I'm a demigod. The miners were right about that particular embellishment in their retelling of the tale, even if they didn't realize it."

"I see. What about Prometheus? Is he a demigod too?"

"No, he's a... well, how should I put it?" Heracles looked puzzled as he searched for the right words.

"Simply," she countered.

"He is a Titan."

"He's what? A Titan? Come now, you cannot be serious. The Titans have been gone for more than a millennium—everyone knows that."

"Do I look like a liar?" Heracles asked, glancing sideways at her.

"No, you do not," Pandora said thoughtfully.

"We're going to need to stop in Abdera. These supplies won't last the rest of the journey. I know a small fishing village along the way—right on the beach. Maybe we could stop there and resupply, if we're lucky and the fishermen had a good catch. If not, we can at least get a decent night's sleep before moving on," he said without looking at her. "May I ask you something now?"

"Of course," she replied.

"That sword at your waist—why do you carry it?" he asked, still looking ahead. "You don't strike me as a warrior. You wield magic, not metal. And the sword looks nothing special besides."

"I know how to use it—perhaps not as well as you, but I can swing a blade if I must. Still, that's not why I keep it. It's a memento. A keepsake from someone close," she said, resting her hand gently on the pommel.

"I thought so. Well, if you ever want to join our daily sparring sessions, just let me know," he said, quickening his pace.

As they neared the village, Heracles paused, his gaze drawn to the deep blue sea. In the distance, the jagged silhouette of Samothrake rose against the horizon, its slopes veiled in mist—as though the island itself resisted full knowing. It was said that Poseidon had once sat atop its highest peak, watching the Thracian Wars unfold to the north. Yet Samothrake was older still—far older—known across the Aegean not for conquest or kingship, but for mystery.

He turned his gaze to the small coastal village, its cottages scattered along the shore in a loose semicircle, all facing the sea. It was a peaceful place, inhabited mostly by fishermen—Abdera's primary suppliers of seafood, since the town sat farther inland, a fair distance from the coast.

Heracles had been here before—a couple of times, in fact. He had even spent a few nights in the village once, alongside Medea. She had taken him fishing one evening—though, unsurprisingly, her method was unlike anything he had ever seen before.

She rowed a small boat just beyond the shallows—never too far from the coast. There, she cast a weighted net into the sea, letting it sink slowly, then dropped a smooth, shiny pebble into the water and waited as it drifted down toward the seabed.

The pebble, catching the faint light from above, drew the curious fish near. And then, when enough had gathered, she snapped her fingers—igniting the stone in the dark below with a sudden, blinding glow. The fish froze, stunned and motionless, as if hypnotized. Finally, she handed him the net's rope and told him to pull as fast as he could, catching the fish before they could recover.

At the small dock where the fishermen's boats usually moored, a larger vessel sat anchored among them, its sails furled against the mast. It looked old but sturdy, with a mismatched timber panel patched into the hull—a sign of past damage, hastily repaired.

The trio descended the hill that separated the main road from the village. As they moved through the narrow paths, they passed cottages with windows and doors shut tight. Only the small, local tavern remained open.

Heracles tossed his belongings onto the soft ground and gestured for Pandora and Prometheus to sit at one of the few carved wooden tables outside the tavern. The door stood ajar, lamplight flickering within.

He stepped into the doorway and raised his voice. "Greetings," he said. "Are you open?"

A young man rose from behind the counter and looked at him, fear clear in his eyes.

"Could we have some wine, if it's not too much trouble? Perhaps a couple of fried or roasted fish to go with it—or maybe some octopus, or calamari?" Heracles asked.

Confusion replaced his fear at the sound of Heracles' courteous tone.

"Wait—you're not one of 'em, are you?" the young man asked, puzzled.

"One of who? Ah—you probably mean the people from that ship, right? No, we just arrived," Heracles said, shaking his head. "Why do you ask? Did they bring trouble?"

"Well... you could say that," the young man replied. Then he raised his voice, tilting his head back slightly—just enough to call over his shoulder without breaking eye contact. "Father!"

Heracles, still lingering at the threshold of the tavern, waited patiently as two older men emerged from the back. One wore a long, stained pinafore; the other was dressed like a fisherman—though with a bit more flair.

"What is it now?" asked the man in the pinafore.

"We have guests, Father," the young man replied.

Both men gave Heracles a scrutinizing look, their expressions a blend of fear and surprise.

"Greetings. Pardon me, but I don't seem to recall your names. What were they?" Heracles said to the men.

“I’m Philemon and this is Menon,” replied the better-dressed one.

“I’m Timon, by the way,” said the young man, gesturing to draw attention.

“Glad to meet you, Timon,” Heracles said with a nod.

“Wait—I remember you,” Menon said. “You’ve been here before.”

“Yes, you’re right,” Philemon said. “I remember you being here, accompanying the Princess of Colchis. Heracles, if I’m not mistaken.”

“Actually, I’ve been here a couple of times. And yes, once it was with the Princess—you remember correctly.”

“What brought you here again?” Philemon asked, his expression now returned to normal.

“Well, a meal would be nice. And maybe a few provisions for the road, if it’s not too much trouble.”

“Regretfully, we don’t have anything to spare,” Menon said—clearly the cook of the tavern.

“How come? Does that ship have anything to do with it?”

“We don’t want to trouble you with our problems,” said Philemon. “Menon, are you sure we cannot spare some food?”

"How about you just tell me what's going on?"

"These damn pirates threatened us—they said if we didn't give 'em our food, they'd pillage the village, kill the men, and take the women and children as slaves," Timon burst out.

Both Menon and Philemon snapped their heads toward him, but before they could speak, they saw the boy's face flushed and burning with fury.

Saying nothing, Heracles turned, walked to their table, unfastened his cloak, tossed it onto the wood, and began making his way toward the dock.

"Where are you going?" Prometheus asked, but Heracles did not reply.

The dock was not far—yet not far enough from what was coming its way.

Several men stood at the end of it, loading wooden crates onto a small boat. They did not notice Heracles until he stepped onto the dock. The planks groaned beneath the weight of his stride, as though protesting each step.

"Oi! Who in Tartarus are you?" one of the men called out, pausing mid-crate.

Heracles did not reply. He simply cast a look at each and every one of them. He counted five.

"Wait—I know you! You're that lump of muscle, dragging that stiff old companion of yours everywhere. You absolute menace—you owe me a hull patch! It took us days to fix the hole you left behind."

"And let's not forget—you killed Kriton. Yes, he was a fool, but he was our fool. A mate, nonetheless."

"You're going to pay for that. Oh, you're going to pay dearly."

"I remember you as well, captain," Heracles said to the same man. "You promised us passage and were paid handsomely—but never delivered. Still, fine. You can keep the armor. Let it cover the damage to your ship... and serve as compensation for the man I killed.

"But do not forget—it was you who started the fight. And if blame is due, it falls on you, the commanding officer."

One of the crewmates began slowly unsheathing his sword.

"Captain, remind that man what happened the last time you lot tried to attack me with weapons in hand," Heracles said, shaking his head.

The captain extended an arm, stopping the man from drawing his sword.

"Look, you aren't killers—I can see that. But you're fools, and worse, you're cruel. You don't deserve death... probably. But you do deserve a reminder. One you'll carry with you for a while—to help you remember not to live as wretched little tyrants.

"Being half-wits—threatening and terrorizing others—is no way to live your lives. So... are you ready?" Heracles said, cracking his knuckles.

The captain and his crew remained still, doubt and fear creeping into their minds. Even so, one of them suddenly charged at Heracles. He swung wide, aiming for Heracles' face—but he ducked beneath the blow, caught the man at the waist, and hurled him over his shoulder. The man crashed hard onto the wooden dock.

The rest of the crew hesitated for a moment—then charged at Heracles. Two of them tried to grab him, but as soon as they came close, he shoved one off the dock and struck the other with a single, brutal punch. The man lost consciousness before his body even hit the planks.

The last crewmate found an opening and punched Heracles in the stomach—only to discover it was like striking solid stone. Heracles caught him by the wrist and twisted until his shoulder popped from its socket, then kicked him off the dock.

The captain stood frozen—silent, and completely still.

In the meantime, the second crewmate who had attacked Heracles clambered back up onto the dock, soaked and panting. He charged again, swinging at Heracles with all he had—but the weight of his drenched clothes dragged him down. Heracles sidestepped with ease, seized him by the back of the neck, and yanked him forward, driving a knee into his stomach. The impact forced a burst of vomit from him before Heracles hurled him back into the sea.

The crewmate behind Heracles came to, slowly pushed himself upright, and drew a knife from his boot. But before he could get close, the blade turned red-hot in his grip, searing his palm with a faint, rising sizzle. With a choked yell, he flung it away; the knife bounced off the dock and splashed into the shallow water, where it hissed in a burst of steam.

Heracles turned and kicked him just above the knee, snapping the joint with a sickening crack. The man screamed, staring down at his grotesquely twisted leg in shock. Heracles silenced him with a punch to the gut, then tossed him into the sea.

“I appreciate the help,” Heracles said to Pandora, who stood a few yards from the dock.

“It doesn’t look like you need it,” she replied with a nod.

With only the captain left standing, Heracles approached and stopped mere inches away.

“Now, captain, here’s what’s going to happen next. I could break a few of your bones, take this boat, and repeat what you just saw on the rest of your men aboard that ship,” Heracles said, his voice low with intensity. “Or you can drag your men out of the water, carry every last crate back to the village, and then leave.

“However, as you might’ve noticed, this is our second encounter. The Known World isn’t as large as it sometimes seems. So if I even hear of you, or your crew, doing anything cruel, vile, or cowardly—I will look for you. And trust me—I will find you. And I will unsheathe my sword.”

The captain nodded rapidly and, without a second thought, did exactly as Heracles had told him. The men back in the tavern watched in confusion as he hauled the crates back, while Timon stood grinning, pointing out where not to place them—waving his arms and shouting, "No, not there—over here, you old fool!"

Once the last crate was in place, the captain gathered his moaning, sniffling crew, climbed into the small boat, and made for their ship.

In thanks, Menon cooked them fish soup, roasted picarel, and octopus, served with fresh bread and a spread of garden vegetables—tomatoes, cucumbers, and onions, all drizzled with olive oil and oregano. Timon did not stop filling their cups with wine, grinning with every pour.

Before they said their farewells, the villagers packed provisions for the road—dried fish, olives, and flatbread—offered with heartfelt thanks and warm smiles.

The whole village came out to wish them safe travels. One little girl rushed forward and wrapped her arms around Pandora's legs, clinging to her as tightly as she could—though her small hands barely reached behind her knees.

With the afternoon sun above them, they made their way out of the village. Pandora paused for a moment and looked back. The people were still waving. A quiet rush of joy welled up inside her—too wide and warm to be named, and so it became a smile.

CHAPTER TWENTY

A TABLE BETWEEN THEM

It took them but a few days to reach the city of Abdera, and, owing to the generosity of the fishermen, they now bore sufficient provisions to continue all the way to Colchis. Yet Heracles, though he typically avoided main roads and populous cities, chose to make a stop there.

He had decided it was time for Prometheus to wield a proper sword. The old Titan was improving—gradually but steadily—with each sparring session, and the wooden stick he carried would serve little purpose in a true fight. Thus, they made for Abdera, the last city of Thrace before their journey turned east—toward Colchis, the farthest of all the known kingdoms.

Abdera was both a stronghold and a city of trade. It stood as the last great outpost before the long road east, fortified with high stone walls and a broad, water-filled ditch encircling its bounds. Though built for defense, it remained open to travelers and merchants—nearly all who passed between the inner kingdoms and distant Colchis found respite within its walls. The city rose from the flat, windswept plains of Thrace, its sole entrance guarded by a heavy metal gate and twin watchtowers built into the wall above the trench.

But it had not always been so. The city had been sacked and burned more than once during the Thracian Wars, and legend claimed it had even been destroyed entirely during the Gigantomachy—the great battle when the gods made war upon the Giants, who met the same fate as the Titans.

Some say that beneath the streets of Abdera lie ancient treasures from that distant time. Yet the king who ruled then feared what might slumber within those relics, and so he had them buried deep, raising the new city atop their resting place.

Despite its storied past, the city was much like most others in the Known World. Its buildings were fashioned from rough stone or pale marble, and its layout followed a familiar order: the agora dominated the center, the barracks stood near the main gate, and the dwellings of its people spread outward in uneven clusters around the market.

Narrow lanes wound between homes and workshops, their walls pressed close, casting long shadows across the stone paths. Vines crept along whitewashed walls and sun-baked stone, clinging in quiet defiance of dust and heat.

Abdera was the only place where one could find such a wealth of weapons and ornaments from distant Colchis. Few cities boasted so fine a collection of gold- and silver-plated blades, their surfaces engraved with curling motifs and inlaid with polished gems that caught the sun like fire. The jewelry was no less exquisite—amulets set with bright stones, earrings shaped like coiling serpents, and rings that shimmered as though they held captured starlight.

Heracles, Prometheus, and Pandora entered the city and made their way toward the agora. Neither of the two questioned Heracles' decision to stop in Abdera.

Prometheus seemed fascinated, his gaze darting left and right as he took in every detail; it was his first time walking through a city of such size and liveliness. Pandora, by contrast, appeared uneasy. She stayed close to Heracles, casting wary glances at the towering buildings and crowded streets, as though the press of people and stone made her skin crawl—though she did her best to hide it.

"I need to visit a place"—Heracles paused—"Why don't you find a tavern or a quiet spot to rest? I will meet you later."

Prometheus gave a quiet nod, and Pandora offered no objection. With that, Heracles turned and walked away, leaving the two of them behind.

"Cryptic," Pandora muttered, glancing at Prometheus, who was still scanning the city around them. "Well then—shall we find something to drink?"

It took Prometheus a moment to respond. "A drink would be welcome."

"Very well. Let us find a tavern," she said, and began walking down the street.

"How about that one?" he asked, pointing to a tavern whose walls were marked with painted red stone.

"Why not? It looks respectable enough," she replied, and the two of them made their way toward it.

The tavern was empty. Only a small cat lingered near the door, licking its paw with methodical care. The sharp scent of roasted green peppers drifted from within. They chose a table beneath the awning and ordered wine. It was dark and smooth, with a hint of fruit beneath the bite of the alcohol.

Pandora's gaze lingered on Prometheus' face for but a moment—yet it was enough to sour the taste of wine on her tongue. For the first time, they were alone. No protector. No watchful eyes. It would be easy to end his life here, in the shadow of the tavern wall. One quick thrust to the chest, and the last Titan would fall. The threat would be extinguished. Their ancient line severed forever.

She hesitated.

She could not do it. Even the thought stirred a flicker of compunction. And though she did not realize it, a flush of color rose to her cheeks—warm and sudden, blooming up her neck and across her face.

She told herself it was nothing—just the heat, just the wine. Yet her fingers had tensed around the stem of her kylix, and her breath had slowed before she realized. The thought of it—the act left undone—clung to her like ash.

"Have you ever been to Abdera before?" Prometheus asked, not noticing her silence.

"No. This is my first time," Pandora replied, her voice steady despite the storm beneath it.

"I like it," Prometheus said softly.

"I can see that. Is this your first time in a city?"

"It is."

"And?"

"Heracles told you about me."

"I asked."

"Do you wish to ask me?"

Pandora hesitated. Then she said, "Is the legend true?"

"What legend?"

"About the divine fire."

"It is."

"Why did you do it?"

Prometheus turned and looked her directly in the eyes. "Because it was right."

"Was it worth it?" Pandora pressed, not shying away from his deep, cerulean gaze.

"It was," Prometheus said. Then he turned away, his eyes drifting once more across the city.

Heracles did not take long to return. He carried something wrapped in a piece of cloth, which he set down on the table with a dull thud.

"This is for you," he said to Prometheus, pushing the bundle toward him.

Prometheus slowly unwrapped the cloth. Inside was a sword—longer than most, plain in design but well-forged. There were no embellishments, no gleam of silver or gold—only tempered metal, shaped for killing. It was perfect for its purpose.

"Time to get rid of that wooden stick," Heracles said, lifting a kylix from the table and taking a sip.

They exchanged a glance, and Prometheus gave a small nod of gratitude. Heracles responded by raising his kylix and downing the wine in a single gulp.

"And this is for you," he said, drawing a freshly forged dagger from beneath his cloak and setting it on the table in front of Pandora. "It will likely serve you better than that old sword you carry."

"I cannot accept this," Pandora said, her voice low, overwhelmed by the gesture.

"You can," Heracles replied. "A small gift, for watching our backs."

"...Fine. I... appreciate it."

"It's nothing," he said, reaching for the amphora to refill his empty kylix.

"How did you even pay for these?" she asked.

"The miners. They gave me a pouch of silver—I even have some left," Heracles said, then downed his second kylix. "Shall we order more wine?"

"What about a bath?" Pandora said with a sharp snort.

Heracles raised an eyebrow. "Are you implying something?" He sniffed under his arm, then recoiled. "Ah. You're probably right about that. To the bathhouse, then. I wager we can get more wine there anyway."

CHAPTER TWENTY ONE
BLOOD AND WINE

Fog, heat, and moisture clung to the chamber of the tranquil bathhouse. Vapors curled above the flickering candlelight, their tendrils dancing as they caught the glisten on the wet stone floor.

The trio sat in separate wooden tubs, each spaced only a few yards apart. All three were submerged in steaming water, rich with scented oils and lather.

Prometheus lay still, silently enjoying the heat, his eyes closed and his head tilted back against the rim of the tub. Pandora scrubbed her skin with focused energy, water splashing around her with each purposeful motion. Heracles, meanwhile, sat with his arms stretched along the edge of the tub, basking in the ministrations of the bathmaids as they worked around him.

The maids smiled and giggled as they tended to him with practiced hands. One worked through the tangled knots of his long hair, revealing the golden hue beneath the grime, and ran her fingers briefly through the dense, unruly beard that framed his jaw—his face handsome even in weariness, with eyes half-lidded in calm. The other scrubbed his broad shoulders and veined arms, her strokes firm as she worked across the hard ridges of his body.

A third maid entered, carrying an amphora of wine, which she set on a small table beside Heracles. She exchanged a glance with the others, and soon all three were giggling. Then, joining in the fun, she crouched and began rubbing his feet—both of which stretched well beyond the edge of the tub, far too small for his size. Not that he minded. In that moment, he was content.

From beyond the door came a faint sound of commotion—one none of them bothered to notice. Suddenly, the door burst open, and a maid rushed inside.

"Bandits! They're attacking the—" was all she managed to say before an arrow struck her in the back, sending her to the floor, gasping for breath through a punctured lung.

The other maids rushed to her side, trying to help—but it was no use. She was already gone.

A man stepped into the chamber—his face wrapped in cloth, his black robes soaked in blood. He took a quick glance around, then raised his blade and leveled it at the maids, who stood frozen in terror. But before he could strike, both of his arms locked mid-swing. He had no time to understand why.

Heracles had already leapt from his tub, water cascading off his massive frame, his manhood swinging between his legs as he charged.

In the rush, his foot struck the small table beside him, sending the amphora of wine crashing to the floor. It shattered, and dark red wine spread across the slick stone, mixing with the bathwater beneath their feet.

He slammed his fist into the man's throat with a sharp crack, crushing breath and bone alike.

The man dropped to his knees, gurgling as blood bubbled from his mouth. He struggled in vain to lift his frozen arms to his neck, drowning on his own blood.

Pandora, calm and focused, lowered her hand.

"There's nothing you can do for her now," Heracles said to the maids as he reached for his clothes. "Find a place to hide."

It took the maids a few heartbeats to overcome their terror before they scattered, disappearing deeper into the bathhouse.

"Are we fighting?" Prometheus asked, dressing as quickly as he could.

Instead of answering, Heracles drew his sword. Prometheus had never seen that look on his face.

Clad only in his tunic, sword gripped tight in one hand, Heracles stepped out of the bathhouse—into a massacre.

Men and women fled in all directions, screaming in panic as masked figures in black—dressed like the one Heracles had just slain—cut down anyone in their path.

The few guards on patrol were quickly overwhelmed, outnumbered and unprepared.

Beneath the pale light of the moon, Heracles moved forward. Prometheus and Pandora followed close behind, their footsteps silent amid the chaos.

The first bandit to approach Heracles died instantly—Teraxion pierced his heart in a single, clean thrust.

The second froze a few steps away, clutching his chest and screaming as Pandora opened and squeezed her fist.

His ribcage collapsed inward, bone splinters shredding every organ in reach.

Heracles ended his suffering with one swift stroke, severing his head from his shoulders.

The bandits finished off the last of the guards and swiftly turned their attention to the trio.

One charged at Heracles, raising his blade high for a downward strike. Heracles deflected the blow and countered with a brutal shove of his lion-headed sword pommel, stamping its shape into the bandit's face.

Prometheus stepped in and slashed across the man's chest.

Reeling but not yet dead, the man made a desperate attempt to strike back—only for Prometheus to answer with another slash, this one ripping his belly open in a horizontal line.

His guts spilled out in wet coils as he fumbled hopelessly to hold them in.

The remaining bandits charged together with a unified cry—one that did little to delay their appointment with the ferryman.

The first of the three lunged at Heracles, swinging in wide arcs.

Heracles deflected the first two strikes and parried the third, throwing the attacker off balance. With a swift counter, he severed the man's arm just above the elbow.

Then he seized him by the throat and pulled him forward into the edge of his blade with such force that the point burst from his back.

Nearby, Prometheus managed to block most of the second bandit's strikes—but one thrust slipped through, locking their blades in a bind.

The bandit pressed forward and drove the point into Prometheus' shoulder.

But Prometheus did not falter. He shoved the attacker's sword aside, and the moment their weapons parted, he dragged his own blade downward and sliced across the man's throat at an angle.

Blood sprayed in a crimson arc as the bandit staggered back, clutching his severed artery.

Across the street, Pandora whispered, "φόβος."

The third bandit began to tremble violently. His hand shook as he tried to raise his weapon against her—but before he could strike, Pandora opened her palm and thrust it toward him.

An invisible force flung him backward into the far wall. He slammed into the stone with a sickening crack, blood splattering against the cold surface as his body sagged and slid down, leaving a smear of red in its wake.

The last bandit stood frozen, panting through fear—uncertain whether to flee or fight.

As Heracles approached, the man raised a war horn and blew hard, releasing a sharp, echoing note.

Heracles drove his sword deep into the bandit's chest, then wrenched it free and, in one fluid motion, carved through his face just below the nose—removing the upper half of his head.

The horn remained clenched between his teeth, the sound fading into silence as his body crumpled to the ground, twitching once before going still.

With the stone slick with blood beneath his feet, Heracles looked around.

The streets were finally silent—no one in sight.

At first, he thought the horn had summoned reinforcements. Then he understood: it had sounded the retreat.

The city was safe, for now. But as he surveyed the carnage around him, he knew the cost had been high.

All the senseless killing twisted a knot in Pandora's stomach, and a wave of nausea rose in her throat—but she forced it down, barely holding herself together.

Prometheus clutched his wounded arm, but the injury was superficial—nothing deep, nothing serious. The look of fascination he had worn that afternoon had vanished, replaced by something far darker: despair.

And Heracles, spattered with blood and entrails, looked neither angry nor sorrowful.

He had witnessed countless acts of cowardice and merciless slaughter—enough, one would think, to leave him numb.

But he was not.

He felt disappointment and guilt—the familiar weight he bore each time he watched mortals turn on one another with such cruelty.

Blunt, thoughtless killing born of ambition, malice, and desperation—the most common diseases of the mortal heart.

Heracles glanced toward the nearest body—a boy, perhaps sixteen, his limbs twisted in a final spasm of fear.

For a moment, he did not move. He did not blink. He let the silence press in, the smell of blood and smoke clinging to his skin like a second layer.

He exhaled slowly, but it did nothing to lift the weight from his chest.

With a sharp, practiced motion, he flicked the blood from his blade—just as he cast off everything he felt.

Regret was never a burden he carried for long.

CHAPTER TWENTY TWO
THE MEASURE OF FEAR

The following morning, Heracles left the town and struck northeast, choosing to track the bandits alone—back to wherever they had come from. Prometheus and Pandora remained behind at his firm insistence.

Both had wished to accompany him, but Heracles had persuaded them to stay and tend to the wounded, saying, "Stay here. We can do two good deeds at once."

The bandits had done little to conceal their tracks, and Heracles followed them toward the mountain range dividing the Aegean from the Black Sea, west of the Sea of Helle.

It took him nearly half a day to reach the forest blanketing the lower slopes of the mountains. He followed the trail deeper into the woods until he came upon a broad clearing along the incline—an opening in the terrain that seemed to slip into the heart of the range.

He spotted a man dressed in black seated by a fire just before the opening. Judging him to be a bandit sentry, he crept forward in silence. The man never noticed him—until it was too late.

Heracles seized him from behind, locking him in a crushing hold between his arms. The man thrashed in shock and panic, but his struggle gained him nothing—consciousness fled him within moments.

With the sentry subdued, Heracles stripped him of his weapons and bound him tightly to a nearby tree. Then he struck him across the face with the flat of his palm, jolting him back to awareness.

The man glanced around, disoriented. "Who… are you? What is happening?"

"Shh." Heracles pressed his index finger to his lips, his other hand resting on the man's throat. "Greetings. You shout—or so much as squeak—and I will rip out your windpipe. Your final thought will be, 'By the gods… he truly did it.'"

The bandit swallowed hard and gave a shaky nod.

"How many of you are in there?" Heracles asked.

"Around twenty now," the bandit replied.

"Are they all armed?"

"Yes."

"Who gave the order to attack Abdera?"

"Kleitos."

"Who is he?"

"Our leader."

"I see. That's enough," Heracles said, reaching for his sword.

"Wait!" the bandit cried—then instantly winced at his own volume. "Pray, wait," he repeated more quietly, shrinking beneath Heracles' intense gaze. "What are you going to do?"

"I'll let you guess," Heracles replied.

"You're the one who killed a bunch of us in the town, right?" the bandit asked, fear wide in his eyes. "Look, the captain—he is mad. He is the son of Ares, a demigod. He kills his own. Feeds them to the dogs if they speak against him. We only follow because we're afraid. I don't want to die... Pray, I do not want to die."

"A demigod, you say? Interesting. Very well. You'll stay here," Heracles said.

The bandit said nothing more. He merely dipped his head, his eyes catching on Heracles' strange gaze as the cloth was tied over his mouth.

Heracles moved through the narrow opening and stepped into a rocky recess—an open space hemmed in by jagged stone, where makeshift tents stood pitched unevenly across the coarse ground, their canvas stained and sagging in the stillness.

The sentry had not lied—two dozen men were gathered at the far end of the recess, all of them armed.

Making no effort to conceal himself, Heracles advanced with heavy, unhurried steps.

One of the bandits spotted him and gave a sharp whistle to the others. As they turned to face him, Heracles stopped a few paces away. They scrambled—some drew their weapons; others froze. None attacked.

"I'd like to have a word with your leader, Kleitos," Heracles said, his gaze sweeping over each man in turn.

The crowd parted, and from the rear emerged a beast of a man. He was as tall as Heracles—perhaps taller—and far broader. Where Heracles' frame was forged of lean, honed muscle, the other was sheer mass: thick-bodied, heavy-limbed, with strength buried beneath layers of size. His arms lacked the clean definition of a warrior's build, but no one with sense would mistake that for weakness. Power pulsed beneath the bulk, coiled and waiting.

"So, you're that scum who butchered my men. You here alone? Where's that witch-whore of yours—and the old sack of bones?" Kleitos growled, shoving aside the last man still in his way.

"I am alone," Heracles said.

"Then you're not just scum—you're also a damned fool. Got anything else to say before we gut you?"

"I challenge you to a duel."

"A duel?" Kleitos recoiled, then let out a groaning laugh—rough and low, like a boar snorting through muck. "You challenge a demigod? Hah! I overestimated you. 'Damn fool' was generous."

Heracles felt nothing. That strange, instinctive pull he always sensed around divine blood—familiar, alien, undeniable—was absent. Kleitos was no demigod. Merely a mortal, draped in the fear of gods like a stolen cloak.

"You know what? I'm tempted to throw them at you—just to watch you tear them apart. Useless swine. Couldn't even take a town in its sleep. I paid someone to open the damned gate, and they still failed. How much easier did I have to make it?" Kleitos spat, his lip curling as he glared at them.

"But..." he continued, voice low and coarse, "it's been a while since I've had a proper duel. And let's be honest—I still need those fools. They owe me a town." He raised his voice. "Isn't that right, you worthless pieces of shite?"

The men lowered their heads, saying nothing.

"Woman!" he barked, and a figure stepped forward—barefoot, tunic faded and worn, a single torn bracelet dangling from her wrist.

"Move your arse and bring me my axe. Now."

The woman could barely lift it—an immense, twin-bladed brute of a weapon—and had to drag it across the stone floor, the metal grinding with every step. Kleitos turned, snatched it from her hands, and struck her across the face. The blow sent her sprawling, blood dotting the ground where she fell.

"I accept your challenge," Kleitos said, hefting the axe and resting it on his shoulder.

Heracles inhaled through his nose, exhaled from his mouth, and drew his sword.

"Let's see what you've got, whoreson," Kleitos snarled—then charged.

He brought the axe down toward Heracles' face, but Heracles slipped aside—the blade struck the ground with a jarring clang. Kleitos roared and swung again, but this time Heracles met the blow with his sword, metal ringing against metal. Blow after blow followed—heavy, wild, unrelenting—yet Heracles held his ground, dodging and deflecting with steady precision.

Around them, the crowd watched in breathless silence.

Kleitos' strikes carried real weight—each one forcing Heracles to meet it with his full strength. Every deflection left no room to counter, only enough time to stay alive. But Kleitos was all brute force: no finesse, no discipline—just raw, unfiltered aggression.

Heracles caught a downward strike and locked the axe low with a swift twist of his sword, forcing both blades to the ground.

For a moment, they stood close, eyes locked—Kleitos' dull, mortal brown, pupils sharp and alive; Heracles' green irises filled the entire eye, glowing faintly with the mark of divinity.

A chill ran through Kleitos—but before the thought could settle, Heracles drove into him, shoulder-first, and unleashed a flurry of short, slicing blows. Kleitos staggered, barely turning aside the strikes—until the last cut caught his arm, biting into flesh.

He stepped back and glanced down at the wound.

Heracles cast a sidelong look at the watching bandits—their faces drawn and silent, wide-eyed with something unreadable. No one moved.

Fury boiling over, Kleitos roared and swung his axe in a wide arc—arms fully extended, feet unmoving. The blade hissed past Heracles' face by inches as he leaned back to evade it.

The overreach left Kleitos exposed—and Heracles answered in kind. With a sharp thrust, he drove the point of his sword deep into Kleitos' shoulder.

But the wound did not stop him—if anything, it enraged him further. He howled and swung his axe in wide, furious arcs at Heracles, who dodged or deflected every strike with ease.

And then, Kleitos saw it—Heracles was holding back.

The thought clawed at the edge of his mind, and doubt crept in—cold and unwelcome—as he kept swinging.

Heracles deflected the last blow and stepped back a few paces. He glanced at the bandits again—faces still empty, still silent—and now he saw it clearly: the sentry had spoken true. They feared Kleitos. They wanted him dead.

Raising his sword high with both hands, Heracles brought it down in a brutal arc. Kleitos raised his axe to block—but the handle split clean in two.

Staring at the broken halves in his hands, Kleitos snarled, stunned, "You'll pay for this, you filthy dog!"—and hurled the lower half of the axe at Heracles.

It struck Heracles in the chest and dropped to the floor with a dull thud. He did not even flinch.

His face flushed with rage, Kleitos charged, swinging what little remained of his shattered weapon.

Heracles brought his sword down with full force, throwing the weight of his entire body behind the strike. The blades met with a violent crash, sparks bursting from the clash—then Kleitos' arm recoiled so hard that what remained of his axe was torn from his grip and sent flying.

Kleitos stood bemused for a single breath—then Heracles, in one smooth, merciless motion, cleaved downward, splitting him from collarbone to pelvis.

Bemusement drained from Kleitos' face, replaced by a flicker of cold understanding—just before his legs buckled beneath him.

Blood streamed from the wound, and for the first time, a shadow of humility flickered across Kleitos' face as he dropped to his knees.

Heracles stepped forward and drove his sword point-down into Kleitos' collarbone, the blade sinking straight along his spine and through his gut.

Kleitos died where he knelt—silent, still, and broken.

Heracles pulled the blade free and wiped it clean against Kleitos' tunic.

Around him, the bandits began to breathe again—their shoulders loosening, faces slack with quiet relief.

Then the woman—now Kleitos' widow—stepped forward and met Heracles' eyes.

"He killed the men who hesitated. Took the women who wept. We followed him, but we never chose him," the woman said, her fingers worrying the torn bracelet at her wrist.

"I was never his wife—not truly. He abducted me after he slaughtered my village. He let me keep this bracelet—it was my mother's. So I would never forget their pain."

Heracles said nothing.

One by one, the men let their weapons fall—some with the faintest flicker of a smile.

The woman looked at him again—not pleading, not angry.

Just free.

CHAPTER TWENTY THREE
IN THE SHADOW OF FIRE

The great eagle sliced through the mist like a blade through softened wax. With wings outstretched, he plunged at a steep angle, his beak cleaving the air as he dove. He burst through the final veil of white—and there it lay: the city of Pantheon, sprawled beneath him in all its majesty.

The eagle veered toward the gleaming palace, where his master awaited in stillness.

"The hour groweth late, Aetos. What tidings dost thou bring me?" said Zeus, his voice calm yet commanding.

Aetos let out a series of sharp cries, tilting his head in sudden jerks, his golden eyes glinting with urgency.

"Thou hast done well. Now, fly." With that, Zeus turned and strode back into the palace's radiant interior.

He passed through vast, echoing halls until he reached a towering door of polished metal—and without a knock, he pushed it open and entered.

"Father!" Artemis said, turning with a start.

"Where is your mother?" he asked.

“I do not know. Probably in the gardens?” she replied. “What is the matter?”

“What about your brother? Do you know where he is?”

“Which one? Hermes? No, it has been a while since I last saw him. What is going on, Father?”

Zeus did not reply. He simply turned and left the room.

“I am well, since you were wondering. Fully healed,” Artemis called after him, her voice light, though the faintest edge of hurt lingered beneath it.

“I know,” came Zeus’ voice from the hall.

Soon thereafter, he reached the courtyard behind the palace, where the royal gardens stretched in serene splendor.

A spectrum of vivid hues blanketed the grounds, as a myriad of blossoms and sacred plants flourished in perfect accord—each one placed with an artisan’s care, as though composed by divine intent. At the garden’s center rose a marble fountain, its basin threaded with veins of gold and silver that shimmered like molten light. From its tiered crown, crystal waters arced gracefully through the air, scattering bright droplets over the immaculate greenery.

Hera sat upon the fountain's edge, her fingers gliding through the shifting waters, drawing forth ripples that danced outward and broke upon the basin's rim.

"Do you know?" Zeus asked, drawing nearer.

"Could you be more specific?" Hera replied, her gaze still fixed on the shifting waters.

"Pandora," he said, the name laden with weight.

"I know." She flicked a ribbon of water from her fingers with quiet ease.

"And?"

"And what? I have faith in her. Embedding herself among them to earn their trust was a calculated move—and the right one."

"I am losing my patience."

"Noted," Hera said, at last turning to face him. "Is there anything else?"

"Where is Hermes?"

"Not here."

"Could you be more specific?" he asked, echoing her words from moments earlier.

"No," Hera replied, tilting her head ever so slightly as the corner of her mouth curved—not quite a smile, but a silent acknowledgment of his mimicry, touched with faint disapproval.

"I do not spy on my children."

"Of course you do not. Fine. I shall find him myself," Zeus said, turning away and leaving Hera to trail her finger once more across the cool, flowing water.

Later that day, a guard rapped at the doors of Artemis' chambers and announced her summons.

Without delay, she darted through the palace's gleaming corridors and stepped into the open air, her gaze drawn toward the workshop, where a thick pillar of black smoke curled into the sky. It rose from the divine forge—a vast structure of stone and dark metal, crowned with slanted roofs and chimneys that hissed and roared like living beasts.

She passed through the heavy metal doors, and at once, a wave of searing heat struck her, pressing against her skin and warping the air into shimmering distortion.

Weapons of every kind adorned the walls—each more exquisite than the last, their polished edges catching the glow of unseen flame.

She moved deeper, into the heart of the forge, until she reached a vast central chamber, where the heat thickened and the pulsing red light threatened to sting her eyes.

Streams of molten fire surged through cast-metal channels, spilling into a wide basin at the chamber's center—a lake of living flame that hissed and churned like a thing alive.

At the center of the chamber stood a broad-shouldered man, bent over a breastplate marked by a single shallow dent, laid upon an anvil of dark metal. His arms tensed with each slow, deliberate strike, firelight sliding over sinew as he corrected the armor's curve. His beard—thick, intricately braided—swung with the motion of his blows, brushing against his rounded belly to the rhythm of ringing steel. As he shifted to examine the metal, his pale red hair, drawn back in a warrior's tail, caught the glow of the forge—neat, disciplined, like the work of his hands.

A woman stood nearby, clad in full armor save for the breastplate—its absence revealing the smooth, unadorned lines of the fitted form beneath, awaiting the final piece. Her long, wavy hair, deep chestnut brown, spilled past her shoulders—a vivid contrast to the pale silver of her war-plate. Through the narrow eye-slit of her helmet, gray eyes—flecked with light brown—gleamed with steady focus. Atop the helmet rose a pale red crest, the lophos, its flame-dulled hue a striking counterpoint to the cool gleam of her armor.

"Athena! You have returned!" Artemis said, her voice bright with excitement.

"Greetings, sister. It is good to see you again," Athena replied with a warm smile.

"Greetings, Artemis," Hephaistos added, his tone a quiet reminder of his presence.

"Forgive me, Hephaistos," Artemis said, inclining her head with respect.

"There is nothing to forgive. I have your new bow ready," he said, his eyes—a blend of red and deep brown—lighting with subtle pride.

"Have either of you seen Hermes? Father is looking for him—and he is not very pleasant about it," Artemis said.

"How come?" Athena asked.

"It is probably about Prometheus."

"What do you mean?" Athena asked, turning her full attention to Artemis.

"Wait, you do not know?" Hephaistos said, glancing at her.

"Know what?" Athena asked again.

"You mean nobody told you? Did you not notice the Nereids were not guarding the gate?" Artemis said.

"I did not come through the gate. I used the underground passage. Now—what about Prometheus?"

"He is free. Heracles broke his chains and took him away," Artemis said.

Athena stilled, her features unreadable.

Then, with measured grace, she removed her helmet, revealing a face not unlike Artemis'—but where Artemis was wild and untamed, Athena's beauty bore the calm of wisdom, the weight of contemplation. She stepped closer, the resemblance uncanny yet tempered by age and bearing, and gently laid her hands upon Artemis' shoulders.

"Tell me everything."

CHAPTER TWENTY FOUR
BLOOD FOR SHELTER

The wind stirred the sparse vegetation scattered across the vast plain, through which the Istros River carved its path. Flowing southward from the desolate borderlands men called the No Man's Land, it hugged the left flank of the Caucasus Mountains, meandering all the way to the Black Sea—opposite Leuce Island.

Colchis lay far in the distance, the end of their journey almost in sight—though many hardships still awaited them.

Heracles, Prometheus, and Pandora moved in unison, side by side, their pace steady and shared. The sun blazed overhead, while the scorched earth baked beneath their feet, and even the air itself seemed to sear the lungs. Dust clung to their sweat-slick skin as the rising wind swept grit across their faces with growing force.

When they reached the banks of the Istros, Heracles dropped the knapsacks onto the dry ground and immediately plunged his face into the cool, shallow water. He drank deeply, his breath bubbling beneath the surface. Then he drew back and exhaled—a long breath of half relief, half pleasure.

The other two knelt to refill their waterskins and rinse the sweat from their faces and arms, while Heracles settled onto a flat stone, tugged off his boots, and sank his feet into the river's cool embrace.

"Do you mind?" Pandora asked, glancing pointedly at Heracles as she knelt by the river.

"What?" he grunted, frowning. Then he followed her gaze to his feet—still submerged in the water just upstream from where she was filling her skin. "Oh. Right." He pulled them out with a lazy splash, shaking off the droplets as if it were no big deal.

"Never mind. I have ingested enough dust to feed me for a fortnight," she muttered, then took a long sip from the skin.

A sudden gust slammed into them, flinging grit into their eyes. Heracles raised an arm to shield his face, blinking hard to clear his vision.

When the blur faded, he saw it—a yellowish cloud on the horizon, rising like a mountain.

A sandstorm. And it was coming fast, rolling straight toward them.

"We need to move," Heracles called out, already pulling his boots back on. "Now!"

"What are we doing?" Prometheus asked, stooping to gather his belongings from the ground.

"We won't be able to see through that storm—and there's no telling how long it'll last. We need shelter, and fast. Follow the river upstream. It leads toward the mountains. Taking cover there is our only option," Heracles said.

"Are you sure?" Pandora asked.

"Unless either of you has a better idea," Heracles said, "this is the only one we have."

Neither offered an alternative, so they turned and followed the river upstream, moving as fast as they could with the sandstorm just a few miles behind them.

The flat terrain and the wind at their backs made the run more bearable—for a time.

Heracles led the sprint, Pandora close on his heels, while Prometheus trailed behind, struggling to keep pace.

They pushed forward until Prometheus caught his foot on a rock and fell hard, face-first into the dust.

The wind howled around them, muffling the sound—swallowing it before it could reach Heracles.

But Pandora heard. She stopped and turned. For a heartbeat, she did not move. She simply stared at him.

Prometheus lifted his gaze and met hers. She stood still, eyes unreadable. But before he could make sense of her hesitation, she rushed forward and pulled him to his feet.

"Come on, old man. This is no time to rest," she said, giving him a gentle push forward.

The sandstorm was at their heels now, and the slopes loomed just a few hundred yards ahead. They pressed on with everything they had.

The wind struck like a hammer, roaring over them and swallowing the world in a storm of dust, leaves, and grit. They pushed forward, straining against the gale, barely able to see more than a few yards ahead.

Every step was a battle, their pace faltering within the curling, shrieking vortex.

Sharp stones tore through the air, pelting their skin with vicious force—like crows pecking at raw flesh.

Heracles was nowhere in sight. Pandora and Prometheus, hands clasped tight, moved as quickly as they could, the river still running beside them. The mountains had vanished into the haze, so they followed the stream, hoping it would lead them to safety.

But it did not.

The storm worsened. Larger debris now tore through the air—splintered wood, jagged stone—each piece capable of ending their journey then and there.

Pandora lifted her head, eyes stinging with sand, and searched desperately for Heracles. Through the blur, she glimpsed trees—barely visible in the choking dust. She gripped Prometheus' hand and pulled him toward them.

A rock whistled past, missing their heads by inches.

They were close now. The trees thrashed like straws in the gale.

Then, through the shifting veil of branches, Heracles emerged and seized Pandora's arm.

"Follow me—quick!" he shouted, pushing forward and nearly dragging them both behind him.

Within moments, they reached the slope, where a wide, naturally formed opening yawned before them. They rushed inside and collapsed against the cool stone walls—battered, breathless, caked in dust. Panting, they fought to steady themselves, lungs heaving in the stale, shadowed air.

"That was close. I thought I lost you for a moment," Heracles said, breathing heavily, bent over with his palms on his knees.

"Yes... you could say that," Pandora managed between sharp, uneven breaths.

Prometheus had slumped against the wall, limbs splayed—utterly spent.

Heracles scanned their surroundings as the storm's howl carried into the cave, dulled but unrelenting. He peered into the darkness ahead, but it swallowed everything. With a grunt, he drew his torch and glanced at Pandora.

"Could you...?" he asked.

With a snap of her fingers, the torch burst to life. She frowned as he stepped deeper into the cave. "Wait—what are you doing?"

"We can't stay here. If something's lurking down there, I'd rather face it than wait here and be cornered with the damned storm at my back,"

Heracles said, already moving into the cave. “So get on your feet—and follow me.”

They moved in tense silence, the cave stretching on as the air grew damp and heavy. Eventually, they reached an opening that led into a chamber—tight, uneven, and just small enough to feel oppressive. Claustrophobic.

Heracles swept the torch in slow arcs, pushing back the dark. Shadows writhed and flickered, making it harder to keep their bearings by the moment. Then he saw it—a narrow tunnel veering deeper into the earth.

The tunnel opened into a much larger chamber, vast and still. Here, at last, they could breathe more easily.

Thin sunrays filtered through cracks high in the rocky ceiling, glancing off rivulets of water that trickled down the walls. Where sunlight struck the stream along the stone floor, it scattered a myriad of shimmering reflections across the chamber—light dancing in silence, painting the space with a strange, gentle serenity.

Heracles paced the edges of the chamber, casting his torchlight across the walls in search of another passage—but found none.

"Well then. Looks like this is it. We wait out the storm here," he said, pressing the torch against the damp wall to snuff the flame.

As the trio shrugged off their gear and provisions, the weight slipping from their shoulders, something shifted in the surrounding darkness—quiet, unseen.

What Heracles had failed to notice earlier were several openings high along the chamber walls—narrow, uneven holes, just wide enough for a man of slight build to slip through.

A faint clatter of falling gravel echoed behind them.

Heracles turned at once, drawing his sword in a single motion—the ring of metal slicing through the silence, sharp and clear against the cave walls.

"We're not alone," he whispered, signaling for the others to stay still.

As Heracles scanned the darkness, eyes began to appear—one by one—glinting faintly in the shifting torchlight. They multiplied, surrounding them, glowing softly in the gloom.

As the shapes crept closer, Heracles could just make out the strange angles of their gaze. Their eyes were shaped like parallelograms—slit and skewed, disturbingly like a goat's.

From the shadows, figures emerged—manlike in form, but wrong in every other way.

Their legs ended in cloven hooves that clacked against the stone with each step. Though their torsos resembled those of men, their hands were grotesque—dark and coarse, shaped like split hooves twisted into the crude semblance of fingers.

And their heads—nearly identical to those of mountain goats—bore horns longer, thicker, and far sharper than any found in the wild.

"Those are satyroi," Pandora whispered. "They are harmless—unless provoked."

"You're half right," Heracles replied. "They're panes—similar, but different. Wilder. More feral." He lowered his sword. "Stay back. I'll handle this."

With the trio backed against the slick cavern wall, one of the panes stepped forward, sniffing the air with slow, deliberate breaths.

"Trespassers," the pane rasped—the word drawn out in a bleating cadence, like the croak of a goat forced into speech. Its wide eyes twitched, narrow pupils jittering erratically as it stared at them.

"We're not here to take your place," Heracles said slowly. "We only sought shelter from the sandstorm."

"Sand. Storm. Trespass. Pay," the pane growled, locking eyes with Heracles.

"Hold now," Heracles said, raising a hand. "There's no need for that. We'll leave at once."

"No. First—pay."

Heracles exhaled through his nose. "Fine. What'd you want? We have some food. You lot like fish?"

"Fish… no. Pay," the pane said, sniffing the air with short, huffing breaths—until its gaze settled on Pandora.

The others followed suit, scenting the air, and began to edge closer.

"Give. Give… her," the pane said, its eyes—like the others'—unblinking, fixed on Pandora.

"What? Me?" Pandora said, her voice tight, skin crawling beneath their stares.

"Yes. Give. The womb. The womb of the old. The womb… of the old blood," the panes echoed, their voices low and rhythmic.

As they chanted, their bodies began to respond—grotesquely, visibly. A primal hunger stirred within them, obscene and unmistakable.

"What are they talking about?" Pandora whispered, recoiling from the twisted spectacle before her.

Their arousal was now unmistakable—bodies taut, breaths ragged, strands of saliva trailing from their mouths as they edged forward.

Heracles stepped between them and raised his sword. The blade caught a shaft of sunlight and flared with reflected brilliance, the sudden gleam halting the panes mid-step as their eyes locked on the divine metal.

"One step closer," Heracles growled, "and I start cutting. I'll take your cocks first, you depraved little beasts."

His voice was like stone—cold, final—as the sword in his grip gleamed with the promise of violence.

The panes did not heed the warning. Their eyes drifted back to Pandora—hungry, fixated.

The first one crept closer.

Then came the sound—a sharp, slicing whoosh—and the creature's head slid cleanly from its shoulders, dropping to the stone with a heavy thud. Its body crumpled a heartbeat later, legs folding beneath it.

The remaining panes screamed—high, guttural wails like goats being slaughtered. And that, indeed, was soon to happen.

"Prometheus—protect her!" Heracles shouted over the rising cacophony, then charged, sword flashing.

He carved through them without pause, slicing and rending, painting the cavern walls in streaks of red.

"I'll give you blood enough to last a lifetime!" Heracles roared, parrying a flurry of horns and claws as the panes swarmed him.

Each counter came in wide, merciless arcs—cleaving heads, severing limbs—in a savage, unrelenting dance of death.

A few panes broke from the chaos and rushed at Pandora—but the moment they neared, they slammed into an invisible barrier.

Their heads snapped back violently, horns shattering on impact, fragments crumbling against the unseen wall of force. Pandora stood firm, arms raised, both palms held forward—the shield flickering faintly with every strike.

Prometheus stood at her side, sword in hand, ready to strike as she kept the panes at bay.

Heracles was fully surrounded now. With each sweeping arc of his blade, multiple panes fell—bodies torn apart, their blood gushing across the stone floor. The ground grew slick with it, the flood turning treacherous beneath their hooves, causing them to stumble as they closed in.

The panes skidded across the blood-slick stone, tripping and crashing into one another—snarling and flailing in the gore.

Heracles made quick work of them, driving his blade into writhing flesh as they struggled to rise.

The panes continued to hurl themselves against Pandora's magic, ramming their heads into the unseen barrier without pause. Their horns were nearly ground to stumps, splintered remnants cracking with each impact.

The other two panes staggered back, pawing at the blood streaming from the broken stumps of their horns, the hot flow blinding their eyes. But the first—the one who had spoken—kept going, slamming itself into the barrier with mindless fury, again and again.

As the two wiped the blood from their eyes and lunged once more at the shield, they froze mid-charge. A faint, rasping cry escaped their throats—then both dropped, lifeless.

The last pane stopped. It turned to Pandora, eyes wide, mouth opening as it let out a piercing goat-scream that echoed through the cavern—

—until a blade drove up between its legs, cleaving upward in a single, brutal stroke.

The scream ended in a wet, gurgling snap as the blade reached its face, splitting it clean in two from groin to skull. Its body collapsed in twitching halves, falling away from itself with a heavy thud.

Pandora stared at the sundered corpse as its halves slumped to the sides—revealing Heracles behind it, drenched in blood from head to toe.

"It is done," he said, exhaling heavily.

Pandora lowered her arms, and the shimmering barrier dissolved.

"Are you unharmed?" she asked, unable to tell through the thick veil of blood clinging to him.

"I'm fine," Heracles said, wiping blood from his brow. "And I know it's far too soon... but does anyone want a pane's cock as a souvenir? I hear they bring luck."

He said it without a hint of a smile.

It was not meant to be funny. And yet, in the silence that followed, they all began to laugh.

CHAPTER TWENTY FIVE

ECHOES OF THE END

Nearly a fortnight passed as they wound their way along the jagged coast and beneath the looming ridges of the Caucasus, the days stretching long and silent. The journey had been uneventful—eerily so, given all they had faced from both mortals and monsters. Each step carried them through a hush that felt too deep, as if the land itself were holding its breath. Yet despite the tension—or perhaps because they were lulled by it—they pressed on.

And then, at last, Colchis came into view—its pale stone walls glinting in the sun, a beacon rising at the edge of the world.

They returned to the very place where Heracles had once paused to rest, more than a year ago—on the hill by the gnarled husk of a withered tree, its twisted roots still clutching the soil where Podargos had stood tethered through the night.

With the sun sinking behind the ridges, Heracles slowed to a stop and suggested they rest here for the night. By tomorrow evening, they would reach the city—and at last, he would lay eyes on Medea and Podargos once more. It had been a long time. Far too long. The thought of seeing them again stirred something unspoken in him.

But not tonight. Not yet.

After weeks on the road, what he needed was rest—a quiet night on familiar ground, before whatever came next.

They set up camp and settled around the fire, the night air still and the sky clear, swept clean of cloud. Overhead, the moon hung bright and full, casting a silver glow across the land—like the gaze of something ancient and unseen.

"Feels strange, being here again after all this time," Heracles murmured, casting a sideways glance at them both.

"Do you mean Colchis?" Pandora asked, her tone curious but careful.

"No," he said, his eyes drifting to the gnarled tree. "I mean this spot. I camped right here before heading into the city." He paused, then let out a short, dry laugh. "Actually, that's not true. They carried me."

"Who did—and why?" she asked again, her brow slightly furrowed.

"You want the long version or the short?" Heracles asked, his voice low with the weight of memory.

"I have nothing better to do," Pandora said with a faint shrug. "The long one."

"Well, I stopped here to rest with Podargos. A patrol of soldiers passed by and started asking questions. We didn't exactly get off on the right foot, but eventually we found some common ground. Then a woman appeared. She claimed the soldiers had pillaged a nearby farm, and said she was there to deliver justice. I told her I could bring them to the King, but she didn't want to hear it.

"Turned out she was a Naiad—what most call a siren. We fought, and she lost. But her sisters showed up during the fight. They slaughtered the soldiers... and Podargos killed them. She bit me during the fight. Her poison nearly finished me. But Medea found me—brought me back. Saved my life.

"That about sums it up."

"Wait—your horse killed the sirens?" she asked, her brows drawn in confusion.

"Oh, yes," Heracles said, his voice light, almost amused. "Podargos is cursed. But unlike

Prometheus here, he can shift into a massive, bear-like beast. Makes him rather useful in a fight."

Prometheus turned toward him slowly, one brow arched and his mouth set in a thin, unimpressed line. No words—just the weight of his silence speaking louder than any reply.

"Come now, I'm only jesting," Heracles said as he clapped a hand on Prometheus' shoulder. "You've come a long way since we started sparring."

"I know I have been a burden on this journey," Prometheus said, his voice low as he lowered his head.

"Nonsense," Heracles said, giving him a solid pat on the back. "You were chained and tortured for a thousand years—give yourself due credit."

Pandora slipped a hand beneath her tunic and drew out the pendant she wore close to her skin, her fingers tracing its edges by instinct.

Heracles glanced over, catching the movement. "What's that? Another keepsake?"

"Yes… something like that," she said, slipping it back beneath her tunic. "I never gave voice to my gratitude."

"For what?" Heracles asked with a small shrug.

"For everything. You have saved me—more than once," she said, meeting his gaze without flinching.

"I just did what anyone would," Heracles said, offering a quiet, genuine smile.

"I doubt that," she replied. "But know that I hold it in highest regard."

"We watch over one another. That is how it should be—simple, really," he said, casting a brief glance at them both before rising to his feet. "Sleep well. Tomorrow's going to test us."

He turned away toward his fur, leaving the two alone in the fire's fading glow.

"May I ask you something?" Prometheus said after a moment's silence.

"Of course," Pandora replied.

"The womb of the old blood—do you know what the Panes meant by that?"

She shook her head. "No. I don't believe so. Likely nothing that would make sense to us. Why bring it up now?"

"I was only wondering," he said quietly. "They kept chanting it before the fight. I cannot shake the feeling it meant something."

The fire crackled softly between them, and a moment of silence passed.

"Rest well," Prometheus said finally as he lay back and turned on his side, pulling the fur over his shoulder.

Pandora lifted her eyes to the moon, and her heart skipped a beat. She did not know what the Panes had meant, yet under that cold, silver light, their words echoed through her mind—distant, yet heavy with some forgotten weight.

That night, she tossed and turned in her sleep, restless beneath the weight of something unspoken.

Snow drifted through the smoke-choked sky, spiraling down in ghostly silence before vanishing against the scorched earth.

Ash curled on the wind like dying prayers.

Beneath the roar of fire rose the screams of the dying—the clash of metal, the splinter of shields, the groan of armor crushed beneath blade and flame.

The sacred city was under siege.

Its marble halls lay cracked and blackened, its golden towers collapsed into ruin.

Olympus burned.

Demigods and mortals battled the gods on the blood-soaked ground of Pantheon, blades flashing and war cries drowned beneath the thunder of destruction. Giants tore through toppled towers, shattering marble halls and hurling gods from the heights like broken idols. Overhead, dragons wheeled and plunged, their wings stirring the smoke as they rained fire upon the sacred mountain.

Together, this impossible alliance waged war against the divine heart of the world.

The gods answered with fire and thunder—lightning speared through the clouds, storms split the heavens, and divine fury rained down upon the invading host.

But the fall had already begun.

It could not be undone.

And on a hill beyond the shattered gates, a lone figure stood.

Tall. Still. Cloaked in shadow, a sword hanging at his side like judgment made flesh.

He watched in silence as Olympus crumbled, its final hour etched in flame.

He was the end.

The harbinger of death.

The one who would unmake the Known World.

Pandora rose without a word, sweat tracing the line of her jaw. She had seen the end—and the end had seen her.

CHAPTER TWENTY SIX

TWILIGHT OF THE FAITHFUL

Long before the sun rose behind the Caucasus Mountains, Heracles was already awake. The others remained in quiet slumber. He stepped toward the old, withered tree and halted at its gnarled roots, letting his gaze drift across the distant kingdom of Colchis.

He still could not believe he had come this far—nor all that he had done. It felt like a dream: distant in time, yet painfully vivid. And still, it was only the beginning.

Through the dim haze of dawn, he spotted movement along the horizon. At first, it was no more than a tremble in the mist—then shapes emerged, sharpened, multiplied. A cavalry unit. A large one. He counted at least twenty riders, their silhouettes bristling with weapons as they closed in.

"Halt!" the lead rider called out, and the cavalry drew to a stop. "You there—state your business!"

"Kleon? Is that you?" said Heracles, descending the low rise and striding toward the captain.

"Heracles?" the man said, lifting his heavy helmet to reveal a familiar face beneath damp curls.

"It is you! How are you, old friend? I missed you last time. A captain now? Hah—fitting, for a soldier who once faced a dragon," said Heracles as he reached him.

Kleon passed his helmet and reins to a nearby soldier, then dismounted in a single, fluid motion. He strode to Heracles and extended his arm. Their forearms met in a warrior's clasp—strong, intentional, and wordless, the kind shared only by those who had bled on the same soil.

"How long has it been? A decade, perhaps?" said Heracles, his voice low with quiet disbelief.

"Longer, I think," Kleon murmured, a shadow passing over his features. "Forgive me, Heracles."

Heracles studied him. "What is it?"

"The King has been hunting for you."

"No surprise there. And Medea?"

"The Princess has been searching for you as well. She rode out nearly a year past and has not returned."

"Then we must send word to her. What of Podargos?"

"We will, once we return. As for Podargos—he is well enough. Growing fat in the royal stables. I passed him this morning."

"Good. I am grateful," said Heracles with a firm nod. "Now, let me guess—you must escort me back to the King."

"I should—but I am under orders to hunt a beast near a mine, a few miles from here. Tell you what: come with us. Lend your strength. A seasoned monster-slayer would be a welcome sight. And I swear, I shall speak in your favor before the King—or at the very least, you shall return with a fresh deed to your name. What say you?"

"Well, it's not much of a choice, is it?" Heracles said, smiling back at Kleon's grin. "Lucky for you, I'm not alone. I've got companions who'll be glad to lend their strength."

"Even better. I look forward to seeing what the friends of a man like you can do in a fight. We've got fresh horses waiting."

"Great. I'll go wake them." Heracles turned to climb the hill, then glanced back. "By the way—you never said. What are we hunting?"

"The reports are vague—but everyone agrees on one thing: it's big."

"Terrific," Heracles muttered, the word flat as stone.

After an hour of riding, they reached the mining village. From a distance, it appeared deserted—silent and still beneath the pale light of early morning.

At Kleon's command, the soldiers broke formation and fanned out along the flanks. He, the trio, and a few others advanced straight down the main path.

Pandora lingered at the rear, as she had all morning. She had barely spoken since waking, her silence stretching with each passing mile.

As they entered the village, they were met with a vision of carnage. Bodies lay strewn across the dirt—limbs torn, entrails spilled, blood soaked deep into the earth. There was no sign of life.

"We're too late," Kleon said quietly, his gaze moving over the massacre. "Spread out. Search the area."

They dismounted and moved in silence, checking the bodies for any sign of life. There was none. Everyone lay dead—even the dogs, their limp bodies steeped in blood.

Heracles knelt beside a corpse. "Fresh kill," he said, eyes narrowing as he examined the wounds. "No more than a few hours old."

"I'll send word to the King. We'll need more men—for the burials," Kleon said, his voice low with grief.

"Wait," Heracles said, crouching beside a trail of smeared blood. "Drag marks."

He followed the trail to a broad, stone-built storehouse. As he approached the half-open doors, a low growl echoed from within—deep, steady, and close.

"It's still here. Get ready for—" Heracles' voice faltered as the doors creaked outward, forced open by a massive lion's head that emerged from the darkness within.

The creature stepped from the storehouse, and at last, its full form came into view. The lion's head at the front was immense— far larger than that of any natural beast—with a tangled black mane and yellowed fangs dripping foam. Its body, too, resembled a lion's, but grotesquely enlarged, its shoulders hulking, muscles rolling beneath a hide marked by deep, faded scars.

From the middle of its back rose a second head—not feline, but goat-like—its twisted muzzle stretched long, the black fur matted with filth. Crooked horns curled outward like shattered bone, and its eyes burned red, gleaming with a dull, malignant glow.

And where a tail should have been, a thick, segmented scorpion's tail arched high behind it—chitinous and pulsing, tipped with a barbed stinger as long as a spear, weaving through the air like a serpent poised to strike.

"Athena protect us—it is a chimera," Kleon whispered, raising his spear and shield.

The soldiers followed his lead, weapons drawn, shields locking into place as they spread out.

Heracles took a single step back, giving the chimera space. Both its heads turned toward them—each locking eyes with a different man. The lion let out a low growl. The goat's head twitched, lips curling. Above them, the scorpion's tail began to rise.

Only a dozen paces from the chimera, Heracles drew his sword and lifted his shield.

"Kleon—I'll draw it in. Order your men to flank it. I'll hold its attention."

His voice was steady, anchored in certainty.

Then he slammed the flat of his blade against his shield—metal striking metal with a sharp, ringing crack that echoed like a war drum beckoning death.

Both of the chimera's heads snapped toward him. In perfect unison, they bared their fangs—one unleashing a deep, shuddering growl, the other hissing through rotted teeth—while behind them, the scorpion's tail rose and began to rattle, dry and furious. The three sounds blended into a single, monstrous cadence: guttural, venomous, and deathly hollow.

"Here we go," Heracles breathed—and surged forward.

The chimera lashed out with one massive paw, claws arcing toward him like blades—but Heracles dropped low, rolled beneath the strike, and slid under the lion's head. In one smooth motion, he drove his sword into its opposite foreleg.

The lion's head bellowed, then snapped sideways as the scorpion tail lashed forward. Its curved barb slammed into Heracles' shield with a bone-shaking thump, driving him back a step—but he held fast. The chimera pressed in, striking again and again, each blow heavier than the last. Heracles grunted through clenched teeth, his boots grinding against the earth as he absorbed the storm.

Kleon and his men hurled their spears in a single, practiced volley—every shaft striking true, driving into the chimera's flanks and halting its assault on Heracles.

The beast let out a guttural roar and twisted violently, ripping the spears from its flesh. Blood slicked its tawny hide as it turned, both heads locking onto the soldiers with renewed fury.

"For Colchis!" Kleon roared, and the charge thundered forward. Blades of darkened metal flashed as soldiers surged into the fight—Prometheus among them, silent and grim.

Pandora remained still as the cavalry swept in from both flanks, hooves pounding, blades drawn, crashing into the fray.

Surrounded on all sides, the chimera thrashed and bellowed—spears biting into its flesh, swords carving through sinew—while Heracles, Kleon, Prometheus, and the others struck with brutal precision.

The chimera's heads roared and snapped, taunting its attackers as the scorpion tail lashed out with deadly precision—skewering two riders, killing them before their bodies struck the earth.

Yet the beast was outnumbered. Blades continued to land, and while most lacked the strength to fell it, the wounds were beginning to mount.

They were winning. They could feel it—and they pushed harder, blades biting deeper, movements faster.

Then, without warning, the tide shifted. The goat head flung upward and let loose a scream so sharp it tore through the air in rippling waves.

The sound was blinding—paralyzing. Soldiers staggered, hands clamped over their ears, faces contorted in pain as the shriek battered their skulls and rang through bone.

And then the chimera struck—with savage fury.

It raked its claws across a soldier, shredding flesh and metal in a single stroke. The scorpion tail lashed next, striking another soldier full in the face—its aculeus bursting out the back of his skull in a spray of gore, then wrenching upward so violently it tore free nearly his entire spine along with his head.

And still, it did not relent. The beast clawed and stung through the ranks, ending lives in a blur of blood and motion.

Heracles, his skull still throbbing from the goat-head's relentless wail, managed to turn and bellow, "Pandora!"

She was too far to hear—but she saw him. And he saw her. Yet he missed the dread behind her gaze.

It was not for the chimera.

It was for something stirring inside her.

A small volley of arrows sliced through the air, a few striking the goat head cleanly. The scream cut off at once.

On a nearby structure, the archers moved with calm precision, already nocking the next shot.

The second volley flew faster—one shaft burying deep into the goat head's eye, making it jerk once before falling still.

The chimera vaulted over the front line, landing hard and crushing soldiers beneath its massive paws as it came down near the structure. With a single sweep of its tail, it tore through the wooden platform—splintering it down the middle. The structure gave way in a thunder of breaking timber, collapsing and burying the archers beneath the rubble.

Heracles, Prometheus, Kleon, and the others were already on their feet. Without hesitation, they fell into formation and charged.

The chimera's tail swept in a brutal arc—skimming just above their heads before crashing into the cavalry behind them. Riders were hurled from their mounts, limbs twisting midair. Some hit the ground hard, bones shattered, jagged fragments tearing through flesh.

With barely a dozen left, they charged—blades carving into the chimera's hide, drawing blood with every strike.

The beast lashed out, claws shearing through metal and meat, rending warriors apart and leaving broken halves scattered in the dirt.

Kleon broke through and drove his sword deep into the chimera's chest—but the scorpion tail darted forward from beneath, striking the instant he struck.

Heracles stepped in, shield raised, just in time to intercept the blow.

The impact was immense. The force hurled Heracles backward—his head slamming into Kleon's face with a sickening crack.

Kleon dropped instantly, unconscious, as Heracles staggered in place, dazed, barely keeping his footing.

The last soldiers, seeing their commander fall, charged in blind fury.

The chimera met them head-on—its scorpion tail plunging straight down, impaling one through the skull and ripping clean through his body, splitting him from crown to spine.

Another gasped his final breath between the lion's jaws. The mouth snapped shut, and with a twist of its head, the beast tore him in half and swallowed what remained.

Prometheus seized Heracles by the arm, trying to pull him back—but it was useless.

The chimera's tail swept across the battlefield, catching them both and dragging them like leaves in a gale before hurling them through the air.

They slammed into the wooden wall of the nearby structure. The frame groaned under the impact, but held—barely.

As they struggled to shake off the daze, the lion head reared up, its bloodied jaws stretching wide.

But before it could taste divinity, Heracles rammed his shield into its upper jaw, and with a roar, drove his sword down through the floor of its mouth, pinning it to the earth—if only for a moment.

The lion head roared back—blood bubbling from its throat. It thrashed to break free.

Heracles gritted his teeth and growled, straining to hold it down.

Prometheus was still stumbling to find his footing as Heracles began to lose ground.

"I cannot hold it much longer—go, Prometheus! Save yourself!" Heracles shouted, muscles trembling as the chimera's jaw began to rise, inch by inch, the earth cracking beneath it.

Then, everything stopped.

The lion head froze, its eyes wide.

"Move!" Pandora's voice cut through the silence.

Heracles ripped his sword from the chimera's mouth and slashed in a wide arc, shearing through the corners of its lips and severing the tendons beneath.

Its jaw collapsed, hanging limp and crooked—flapping uselessly like torn hide.

Without pause, Heracles seized Prometheus and pulled him back toward Pandora.

Her hands trembled as she raised them, straining to hold the chimera in place—but it kept pressing forward, relentless.

She pushed back with everything she had, but the beast would not yield.

With a grunt, she turned her arms. The lion head, its ruined jaw dangling, mirrored her motion.

With a cry, she twisted.

A crack split the air as the lion's neck snapped sideways—broken in an instant.

Heracles and Prometheus dropped to their knees, mere yards from Pandora, watching as the chimera's legs gave out and its body collapsed in a final, shuddering heap.

"How did you do that..." Heracles began—but then the feeling hit.

A deep, primal pull surged through them both—that strange awareness they had always sensed in the presence of divine blood.

Familiar. Alien. Absolute.

But the pull was not from each other.

It was from Pandora.

Her illusion had shattered the moment she revealed her true divine magic.

"Pandora?" Heracles murmured, eyes fixed on her, stunned.

"Forgive me," she said softly, sorrow deep in her gaze—just as the scorpion tail snapped toward her.

She caught it—just in time.

But the tip of the aculeus had already grazed her skin—just enough for the venom to enter.

Prometheus lunged, his blade sinking deep into the tail—but not deep enough to sever it.

Heracles followed an instant later, cleaving it off with a single, final blow.

The severed tail hit the ground and twitched, spasming in jagged bursts—until Heracles stepped forward and drove his sword through it, pinning it still.

What remained of the tail flailed and shook, flinging blood in wild arcs as the chimera began to rise once more. The lion head hung limp, dragging lifeless through the dust. But the goat head still lived.

"Enough," Heracles growled—and charged.

As the chimera staggered upright, Heracles slipped beneath it and plunged his sword right under the lion's throat—then, with a snarl of exertion, dragged the blade down through its underbelly, carving a single, merciless path.

Warm blood and entrails spilled from the gash, drenching him from head to toe as he tore the blade free and stepped aside.

Blood streaked his eyes, blinding him just long enough to misjudge the fall.

The chimera's corpse collapsed sideways, slamming into him and trapping him from the waist down beneath its massive, lifeless bulk.

Heracles cried out, forcing every ounce of strength into his limbs—pushing, straining—but the carcass did not budge.

Prometheus stepped forward to aid Heracles—

—but the unmistakable hiss of a blade being drawn behind him froze him mid-step.

He turned.

Pandora stood there, her face drained of color, breath faltering, sweat streaking her brow.

In one hand, she held her ordinary sword.

The other remained outstretched, fingers trembling, still holding the chimera's corpse in place.

"What are you doing? He needs help!" Prometheus said, though a gnawing dread had already begun to take hold.

"I have no choice," Pandora said, her voice barely a whisper, trembling as she fought to hold the spell together.

"Why?"

Pandora raised her sword and stepped forward.

She swung at Prometheus—but he caught the blow above his head, locking her blade with his own.

"Stop this," he said, driving her back and knocking aside her weapon.

"You will end everything. I have seen it," she cried, and struck at him again with trembling hands.

Prometheus turned his blade, deflecting the blow with ease.

"They lied to you," he said quietly. "Do you even know who you are?"

"No," Pandora breathed, a tear tracing down her cheek. "They raised me. You killed my parents."

"No, Pandora. I have not," Prometheus said, deflecting another of her strikes with a sharp clash of blades. "Who told you that?"

"Hera—she told me everything," she gasped, her face contorting as she fought to hold back her emotions.

"I do not—" her voice broke, and she forced the words out. "I do not want to do this."

"Then stop!" Prometheus thundered.

Heracles could not see them—but he heard the clash of blades, sharp and relentless, ringing through the air.

"What in Tartarus is happening? Are you going to damned help me or not?" he bellowed from beneath the chimera's carcass.

Heracles had had enough.

Gritting his teeth, he heaved upward, pushing with all his strength until the chimera's carcass shifted—just enough for him to crawl free.

Agony flared through his leg. It was broken. But he could still move.

With a groan, he dragged himself upright and began limping toward the sound of clashing metal.

Then he saw it.

For a moment, he could not believe it—

Prometheus and Pandora, locked in combat.

"Stop this—both of you!" Heracles shouted.

Pandora turned, saw him, and lifted her hand—locking him in place with a flick of her fingers.

"What do you want, Pandora? Truly?" Prometheus asked, catching her next strike with his blade.

"I... I do not know," she whispered, blood slipping from her nose. "Only that you must die.

"It is either you—or everyone else."

With her strength fading, Pandora released Heracles—if only for a breath.

In a single, fluid motion, she flicked her wrist and disarmed Prometheus, sending his sword spinning through the air.

Then she thrust her hand forward—and he was hurled backward, crashing onto his back a few paces from Heracles, who had limped forward as far as his shattered foot would allow.

"Enough!" Heracles roared, now standing beside him.

But before he could reach Prometheus, Pandora froze him once more—blood now smeared across her face, pooling at the corners of her mouth.

She lunged at Prometheus, sword angled downward. As she moved, her dagger slipped from her belt and clattered to the ground.

Prometheus caught the descending blade with both hands, halting it inches from his chest.

And then he saw her eyes—truly saw them—and the truth buried inside.

"You are a Titan," Prometheus said, straining to hold the blade back as blood streamed between his fingers.

“Lies!” Pandora spat, driving the sword down with one hand while her other kept Heracles frozen in place.

“Pray stop!” Heracles pleaded, his voice ragged with desperation.

“You are a Titan… and a god,” Prometheus said, his voice low, the blade slipping from his blood-soaked hands. “I see it now. I heard the whispers—but never thought them true.”

“Why would they lie?” Pandora asked, her tears carving lines through the blood on her face.

The sword trembled in her grasp, as if her own essence recoiled from the act.

“Because they would never allow such a union. Not after the fall of our kind. They fear us… Sister,” Prometheus said, as the blade grazed his skin.

“Pandora, I beg you—stop! Do not do this. It is not you!” Heracles cried, forcing himself forward against the dying grip of her magic. “Pray, let him go!”

“They used you, Pandora," Prometheus rasped, "forged you into a blade against your own blood.”

“No… no. No.” Her voice cracked. “You lie. They raised me—as one of their own.

“And I saw you—destroying Olympus.”

She trembled. "No… forgive me."

And with the last of her strength, she drove the sword down.

As the blade sank into Prometheus' flesh, it flickered—distorted—

and the illusion shattered.

A pulse of ancient power surged up the hilt, and Pandora knew it—felt it in her very blood.

The true weapon revealed itself: not wrought by mortals, nor shaped by gods,

but forged in the age of Titans.

The blade that had once belonged to Prometheus.

"I only wish you had chosen to believe in yourself," he whispered, as his eyes fell shut.

"No…" Heracles breathed. "What have you done?"

His voice broke. "No. No… no."

Pandora, grasping at last the shift in the tide, lifted her head and looked to Heracles.

"Was… was he telling the truth?" she breathed. "What have I done…"

Something broke open inside Heracles.

He pushed forward, tearing through the last threads of her fading magic.

"How could I have known?" she said, her voice low, thick with regret.

As Heracles reached her—his breath ragged, eyes burning—she lowered her hand.

"Forgive me," Pandora whispered.

With a cry ripped from the depths of his chest, Heracles seized the fallen dagger and plunged it into her heart—hard, fast, without mercy.

He grabbed her by the head, teeth clenched, and with a brutal twist, snapped her neck.

Silence followed.

Even the wind seemed to wait.

Her body collapsed over Prometheus, her cheek settling beside the sword still lodged in his chest.

The last light in her eyes dimmed—

and shimmered briefly across the blade's ancient metal.

Heracles dropped to his knees beside them, breathless, broken—

as Pandora's body began to fade.

Ashes lifted from her skin, carried off by a warm current of wind,

until nothing remained but her clothes—

and the pendant: a small cube, resting silently in the dust.

It pulsed once—faint, steady—

then vanished in a blink.

Heracles stood motionless, his mind adrift—clouded by fury, grief, and the hollow silence left in Pandora's wake.

He did not know what to do.

He only knew this:

Something had broken inside him.

EPILOGUE

In the divine city of Pantheon, within its hallowed halls, a sudden pulse of ancient power stirred, sending invisible ripples across the entire Plateau of the Muses.

In the very chamber where—not long ago—Pandora had been entrusted with Prometheus' sword, the air writhed and coiled, drawn irresistibly toward a shimmering, transparent void at its heart.

The shimmer pulsed—once, then again, and again—each throb quivering with unseen might.

The great doors parted with a low groan, and Hera strode into the chamber. At once, her eyes fell upon the shimmer, suspended above the central table of her sanctum.

The invisible shimmer continued to draw the air inward, its pull stirring loose scrolls and delicate tools scattered across the chamber. With a sharp snap of her fingers, Hera cast the room into darkness.

Slowly, the shimmer coalesced, sharpening into the outline of a hovering, cubic vessel above the table.

The vessel throbbed—each pulse quickening, each surge striking harder than the last.

Hera advanced, lifting her arms high. She spread her palms wide and, with a sovereign gesture, thrust her hands toward the vessel. Yet as she strained to make contact, the relentless waves of power drove her back, denying her touch.

She pressed harder, her fingers quivering beneath the immense force radiating from the vessel. Ancient incantations poured from her lips in a hoarse whisper, their power raking at the rhythm of the pulses—slowing their unyielding beat.

Summoning every shred of her strength, Hera lunged forward, her fingertips a breath from the vessel. Then, with a furious burst, the vessel unleashed a shockwave, hurling every loose object across the sanctum and smashing them against the distant walls.

Hera barely withstood the blast. Gathering the last of her strength, she lunged once more for the vessel—yet it was already too late.

Fresh streaks of white threaded through her hair.

The vessel shattered into countless gleaming specks, the fragments hanging in the air like ghostly mist before slowly dissolving into nothingness.

Only a single speck remained—so small that even Hera's keen eyes could not perceive it. It hovered for a heartbeat, then darted through the open doors.

It slipped through the halls of the divine palace and soared beyond the city, drifting southward.

It swept over the green plains of Thessaly, where herds of white oxen grazed beneath the golden sun, and over the sacred town of Delphi, where thin columns of smoke curled from ancient altars.

It glided between the shadowed cliffs of Mount Parnassus and the shining roofs of Thebes, then soared across the gleaming waters of the Korinthian Gulf, where dolphins leapt beside the passing wind.

It passed above the lush forests of the Peloponnesus, stirring the misty canopy as it drifted over Nemea and Lerna—before descending farther still.

Brushing past the rugged hills of Sparta, it made its way to Cape Tainaron—the furthest edge of the mainland, where the Known World yielded to the endless sea.

From there, it continued to the tip of the Mani Peninsula, slipping into a narrow cave hidden among jagged rocks.

At the cavern's end, the speck plunged into a bottomless pit, descending through endless darkness until it spilled into a vast expanse cloaked in mist and eternal shadow—the Under World.

It drifted through the sorrowful mists, gliding above the black currents of the River Styx and past the shadowed thresholds of the Asphodel Meadows, Tartarus, and the Elysian Fields—until it came upon a yawning abyss.

Then it descended once more, plunging into depths where not even the dead dared tread, until it reached a vast chamber shrouded in gloom.

At its farthest edge stood a towering gate, its blackened surface swallowed by shadow.

The speck drifted closer, its motion slowing as it neared the threshold.

It hovered for a breath, pulsed once with a feeble light—then vanished into the darkness.

END OF BOOK TWO

Stay Connected

We would love to keep you updated on upcoming books, special editions, and exclusive content related to *The Last Titan* saga. To join our mailing list or for any inquiries, please contact us:

Email: info@the-last-titan.com

Website: www.the-last-titan.com

Patreon: www.patreon.com/HephaistosWorkshop

Social Media

Facebook: www.facebook.com/TheLastTitanOfficial

Instagram: www.instagram.com/TheLastTitanOfficial

TikTok: www.tiktok.com/@TheLastTitanOfficial

X (formerly Twitter): www.x.com/TheLastTitanX

Thank you for your support. We hope to see you again on this journey as the saga unfolds.

MAY ATHENA LIGHT THY PATH AND GRANT THEE WISDOM

www.ingramcontent.com/pod-product-compliance
Lightning Source LLC
LaVergne TN
LVHW091108080826

845145LV00008B/1850
9786180060164